DEMON IN THE SAND

The moving sand mound, now only a hundred feet from the goat, must have made some sound because the animal suddenly raised its head and turned. It bleated once and tried to back away, but the mound accelerated, and suddenly two long snaky tentacles came up from the sand and wrapped themselves around the helpless goat. The goat screamed, and then the tentacles dragged it down under the surface.

Whatever was under the sand was either eating the goat right there or it was going back deeper, because there was no movement now, no mound skimming just under the surface.

Durk made it over the fence in one step and then ran toward the truck. He didn't remember opening or closing the door. He was just suddenly driving like hell back across his fields. Good, solid clay fields where no sand-demon could go.

Other V books from Pinnacle

V

THE CRIVIT EXPERIMENT

Allen Wold

PINNACLE BOOKS NEW YORK

V: THE CRIVIT EXPERIMENT

Copyright © 1985 by Warner Bros. Inc.

An original Pinnacle Books edition, published for the first time
anywhere.

First printing/May 1985

ISBN: 0-523-42466-3
Can. ISBN: 0-523-43441-3

Printed in the United States of America

PINNACLE BOOKS, INC.
1430 Broadway
New York, New York 10018

9   8   7   6   5   4   3   2   1

THE CRIVIT EXPERIMENT

Chapter 1

There was no moon, and what little starlight there was was blocked out by the dense foliage overhead. The four figures moved through the trees of the Park, close enough together that they wouldn't lose each other. It was easy keeping quiet here, where the Park forest was tended, but as they went south they passed beyond the area under management and entered the part that was still as it had been when the Research Triangle Park had been developed years ago.

Here there were briars, brambles, and other vines, including poison ivy. Mark Casey, the only one with any combat experience, led the way by dead reckoning. Though they all knew where their destination lay, none had ever been there, nor had they traveled this route before. Humans were not welcome at the research complex which the Visitors had taken over from General Electric six months ago.

It was only a little after midnight, still early for the kind of exploit on which they were engaged. But unlike the raids that still occasionally got TV coverage, this trip to what was now the Visitor RTP Area Administration Center would fail utterly if it was even suspected to have taken place. They were not going to attack, to fight, or to destroy, but to spy.

Behind Mark was Lester Ortega, short and dumpy compared to Mark's tall, slender frame. He kept his hand gently on Mark's back, to keep track of his leader's position.

Separation of more than a few feet would lose him in the dark. Behind him was Steve Wong, not much taller than Lester, but thinner even than Mark, his body hard and stringy. Behind him came Anne Marino, taller than the two men in front of her, her eyes and ears directed to either side and behind, letting herself be led by her hand on Steve's back.

They did not speak as they walked, nor when they stopped at the edge of the untended area. Ahead were more trees, mostly pines sixty or so feet tall, but the ground was a carpet of pine needles instead of a tangle of undergrowth. As they had rehearsed it back at the woods surrounding the Data Tronix building to the north, they came up beside Mark and leaned toward him so that they could hear his whisper. This was just in case the Visitors had sound detectors aimed in their direction.

Mark was peering through the subtly lessened darkness, trying to locate their position. An occasional star peeked down through the pine branches high overhead. The ground sloped gently down toward the south, and he thought he could see a denser area to his left, which should be the shallow bed of a run-off creek, dry except after a heavy rain. If that was correct, then he knew where he was. He'd studied the topo maps of the area carefully, though it was different actually being there.

He hunkered down on his heels, and the others did likewise. That close to the ground, their soft whispers should be distorted by the ground itself and not recognizable if they were being listened to.

"If we're where I think we are," he whispered, and the others had to lean nearer to hear him, "the GE building is just over a rise ahead. Spread out a little bit, try to keep your neighbor in sight, count two hundred paces, then stop."

They did not vocalize their response, but stood up again, forming a line to right and left of their leader. Lester took the far right, then Mark, then Steve, with Anne on the far left. She had the better night vision, and so was given the flank where there was more likelihood of running into trouble with undergrowth. They spread out until they were about ten feet apart, and barely visible to each other.

Mark made a small sound with his mouth, a kind of kissing noise that might have been a bird or an insect calling. With that signal they set out, trying to keep a straight course, and keeping as quiet as they could. Silently they counted. At seventy-five, by Mark's count, the ground began to rise gently, though the hill ahead of them was invisible. At step one hundred eighty-three, the shallow slope leveled off, and he stopped at two hundred.

He looked around. None of the others were in sight. Once again he made the small noise, and heard Lester responding from his right. Cupping his hands, he chirped toward the left. Steve answered, and then chirped again, a predetermined signal that Anne, farther away, had seen something. Mark chirped back at Lester, waited until the smaller man joined him, and then went toward his left flank. Occasional chirps kept them on course.

Their line had lengthened considerably in the short march, and Anne was fifty paces left of Mark's position. She was now lying on her stomach, peering across the top of the ground toward a tiny spark of light off through the trees. Since the Visitor center was the only building in this part of the Park, that had to be what was ahead of them.

They paused a moment, to calm themselves, to focus their attention, and on Mark's signal they started toward the light. Though they now knew where their destination lay, they still had to keep track of each other. And they had to be more quiet than ever. They didn't know if the Visitors had sound detectors aimed in their direction, and they had to be careful of the possibility.

The tiny light ahead flickered as they moved, now blocked by a tree, now revealed again. It grew lighter, and then there were other lights visible. Abruptly they came to the edge of the tended forest, and bare lawn swept down to what was supposed to have been the General Electric research facility, before the Visitors had come nearly two years ago, and which had stood empty for a year and a half.

Far off to the left they could now hear the faint sounds of traffic on the highway that ran south from Durham past the east side of the Research Triangle Park. Trees there obscured the headlights of the few cars going by. Trees beyond the Visitor center formed a black shadow, higher than the facility itself, so that they could not see its outlines. To the right of the building were the parking lots, intended to serve a staff of five hundred, now holding only four skyfighters in various configurations, and a half-dozen ground vehicles.

And halfway between them and the building were the pale blue horizontal lines of an energy-beam fence. But Mark was prepared for that. After a silent consultation with his fellows, he started across the lawn, crawling on his stomach. One by one, in single file, the others followed him, being careful not to dig into the rough turf and thereby leave any tracks.

The light of the energy fence was bright enough to see by. Each beam, as big around as a quarter, was separated from the next above and below by only ten inches. An occasional insect sparked to destruction as it touched the pale blue light. A small explosive charge could destroy one of the pylons from which the beams emanated, but that would give them away and might not even give them access.

Instead, Mark took an object like a long, flexible vacuum cleaner hose from Steve's back. At each end was a large lens, covered with a lens cap and attached to a short, sharp spike. Mark inched up to the fence, placed one spike into the ground, and pushed it down until the lens was at the same height as the lowest beam. Then, moving to the right, he placed the second lens similarly. They were just far enough apart so that he could reach both lenses at the same time. He took off the lens caps, and then with one quick movement pushed both lenses into the path of the beam at the same time.

If the beam were broken for longer than it would take for a rabbit or bird to be destroyed as it passed through it, an alarm would sound inside the building. He had that much leeway. The light of the beam entered one lens—he didn't know which one—and was fed through the massive fiber-optic bundle encased in the tube connecting it to the other lens. They now had a clear space about three feet wide, with the next beam up twenty inches from the ground.

From Lester's back Mark took a second light pipe, this one with longer spikes, and performed the same operation, shunting this second beam around as he had before. One more light pipe from Anne's back, and they had a clear space wide enough for one person, and high enough to let that person go through in a low crouch instead of a crawl. The light pipes were long enough that they could be pulled well back and out of the way of anyone trying to go through this seeming hole in the fence. Mark was first.

They left the three rerouters in place, in anticipation of their departure. Staying low to the ground, they moved closer to the building. There were no spotlights illuminating the grounds, just the faint glow of several windows on the first and second floors. Just a few windows—with a staff of about twenty, most of the building was left empty.

But there were guards, at least two of them. Their posture and walk as they patrolled indicated that they were expecting no trouble. Mark and the others intended to give them none. It would have been easy to sneak up behind one of the Visitors and slit his or her throat, but a body, or even a missing guard, would have alerted the Visitors that someone had come here, and that would have defeated the purpose of this expedition. For the plans to work, the Visitors couldn't even suspect that any humans had been near tonight.

It was Steve's turn to lead. He took out a tiny map, its markings dead black on a super-white surface so that he could read it if there was any light at all. He waited until the guards were out of sight around a corner of the building, then led the others toward a loading bay at the other end of the structure. But as they neared, they could hear the strangely resonant voices of the Visitors.

There was no concealment. Steve made his decision

quickly and scuttled across the lawn to where concrete traffic stops at the edge of the parking area cast a slightly deeper shadow, and threw himself into its dubious protection. The others followed suit. Only the brighter light of the guard-post area protected them, making the Visitors' eyes less sensitive than they might be to the dark. They did not wear their dark glasses here, since this level of illumination was what they preferred. Had the guards been standing in a darkened alcove, they could have seen the invaders easily.

The four humans put their heads together so that they could see Steve's map. He pointed to the place on the sketch that corresponded to the loading dock by which they had intended to enter, and then to another place, farther around toward the side of the building. The front faced south, and they were at the north. At the side were several other entrances, which under normal circumstances would have been lit up at night. Even if they were tonight, they had to take the chance, because there was no getting in the way they had planned.

To get to the other possible entrance, they had to cross the parking area. This was paved with gravel, and it made a lot of noise as they walked, but in compensation, they were able to hide behind the flyers and ground cars. The alternative entrance was in fact dimly lit, but there were no Visitors in sight. They waited until the guards came around, ambling easily and talking softly to each other. When they passed the corner on their way to the guard station, the four humans went quickly to the slightly recessed door.

Mark got out the key that had been specially made for this expedition and tried it in the lock. It entered perfectly, but wouldn't turn.

"Let me," Anne whispered. Mark made room for her at the door.

She took a small bundle from her jacket pocket, including what looked like a pair of glasses. When she put these on, twin pencil-thin beams of light shone out, crossing just inches in front of her eyes. She knelt at the door so that the lights illuminated just the lock itself and no more. Then she took two dental picks from the bundle and inserted them in the lock.

"They teach you more than physics and computer science at Caltech," she muttered as she worked. Her right-hand pick sought the tumblers, the one in her left hand held them in place as she lifted each one. At last she seemed to be done. Mark reached over her head and delicately turned the knob. The door opened, Anne withdrew her picks, and they all went inside.

"Don't let the door close," she hissed as Steve came through last. He caught it just in time. Anne wiggled the inside knob—the bolt stayed shut. She pressed it in and with a bit of adhesive tape fastened it tight. The outer knob would still feel locked, and the regular latch would keep the door closed, but from inside they would be able to open it easily.

"Good," Mark said as Anne let the door close at last. Then he turned to Steve. "Where are we?" he asked.

Steve took out another map, a larger one more prosaically printed. On it was a complete plan of the ground floor of the GE building, now the Visitor RTP headquarters.

"This is the shipping department," he said, pointing. "See, right there are the loading docks and the warehouse areas, but here is where all the offices are for that." He traced a line with his finger. "We have to go through here . . . and there're the stairs to the basement."

"You lead," Mark said.

The inside of the building was pitch black once they left the immediate area of the door. As they had in the woods, they went single file, hands on the person ahead, while Steve led the way by feel and by his memory of the map. It seemed to be going well until Steve suddenly stopped.

"I've got to have a light," he whispered. They clustered around him so the beam from the dimmed flash that Anne held wouldn't shine farther than their own bodies. Steve looked at the map, looked around at the room in which they now found themselves.

"They've changed the partitions in here," he said. He

checked the map again. "It looks like they've divided the stock area up into smaller rooms. I have no idea where the stair is from here."

"Is there another way down?" Lester asked, fidgeting nervously.

"There's a central stair just beyond the shipping offices," Steve said. "We'll have to go back to where we came in."

"Well, let's go then," Mark whispered. "It's after two."

"Let me memorize the map a minute," Steve whispered back. "Okay," he said after only a few seconds. "Lights out, follow me."

He led them back to where they had entered, and then into the darkness again. Up a hall, into a large room which they traversed by going along the wall, out a door, and into another space, which, they could tell by the sound, was large and empty. From somewhere came the muffled sound of voices. Steve hesitated a moment, then turned them toward the left. Mark, immediately behind him, heard him fiddle with a doorknob, and then felt Steve's shoulder lower as he started down a flight of stairs.

At the bottom Steve asked for light again so he could check out the basement floor plan. They did not speak, and it took him only moments to decide where they were and which way to go. He led them on, into an area where there were dim lights shining in the ceiling. Even Visitors could not see in absolute darkness, and the lights here indicated that this part of the building was occasionally visited.

They went down corridors, across what looked like a handball court, past showers and lockers, and through a heavy door into another hall. "This is where we should have come down," Steve whispered, pointing to the right, where a stairway descended from the floor above.

They moved quickly now, having rehearsed this route before. The corridor lights were very dim, but there was enough light so they could see where they were going. Steve paused at another heavy door, a security door, where once again Anne went to work. She quickly had it open and they all went inside.

This door opened with a simple press bar from within, and when it was shut, sealed off all light. In the pitch blackness Anne felt for and found the switch.

"This is the right place," Lester Ortega said as the lights came on, nearly blinding them though these lights too were set for the aliens' preferred lower illumination levels.

It was a small room, with heavy power buses set into the walls, wires and cables of all kinds coming down conduits to boxes, breakers, panels, and connectors. This was the heart of the building—all electrical lines joined here in a giant ganglion before being sent out to the world or in to offices and stations inside.

Once again it was Mark's turn to take command, as Anne kept an ear to the door. Though no light could get out, sound might, and if she heard anybody in the hall beyond, she would turn off the lights and all would fall silent.

Mark compared the panels, boxes, and buses with a diagram he took from an inside pocket while Steve and Lester looked on. "Dammit," he said, "they've changed more than just a few partitions."

"This is the main power bus," Lester said, not quite touching a heavily insulated cable.

"I know that," Mark snapped, "but what is all this stuff?" He gestured at a square yard of switches, connections, and dials of obviously alien manufacture. "These spec sheets don't do us any good."

"As long as we find the main phone line," Lester said, "I think we can still pull it off." He took out a lineman's headset and started gingerly applying the alligators to pairs of likely wires.

As he worked, Steve and Mark started tracing other wires, comparing them to their now useless spec sheets. By the time Lester found what he was looking for, they had tentatively identified several of the other lines they had wanted to patch into.

"Start taking covers off," Lester said, putting the headset away. He took off his pack and took out dozens of fine insulated wires in twisted pairs, each one with a piercing connector at one end and a tiny jack at the other. He himself removed the panel from what he had identified as the phone lines, not a typical phone connection but a heavy-duty switching panel which provided a dozen outside lines.

Working with Superglue, he mounted a tiny jack panel behind the main switching structure. Then he went from one bus, box, and line to another. At each, he fastened the spike of a hair-thin tap wire through the insulation, and led the other end to his jack panel.

"Do you have enough wire?" Mark asked, closing one panel after Lester had finished.

"Plenty. We were planning on twenty connections, so I brought a hundred pairs."

Lester knew exactly what he was doing. The wires he placed could not be concealed, so Steve disguised them by wrapping them in a split flexible conduit the size of a pencil, and fastening it to the wall with staples which he glued in place rather than driving into the concrete. When he was finished with one bundle, it looked just like it was supposed to be there. Anyone not intimately familiar with the layout would assume it was part of the overall design.

It seemed to take an agonizingly long time.

In another part of the building, on the second floor, the lights were much brighter, and there were plenty of people moving about without fear of discovery. But, then, these were aliens, the Visitors who now owned this building, from which they monitored, directed, and administered the entire Research Triangle Park area of central North Carolina.

In an office once intended for the GE research administrator, three Visitors sat in front of a huge desk, behind which sat Chang, a tall woman who was the current Triangle Area administrator. Her Chinese features were handsome and strong, but there was a trace of tired frustration in her expression. She had hoped to serve in a more exalted capacity than here in this backwater, no matter how potentially valuable Diana and the planetary coordinators thought it might be.

"I hope your flight was uneventful," she said to the simulated black man who sat directly across from her.

"A little traffic near the airport," Leon answered, "but we expected that." The Raleigh-Durham airport just east of the Research Triangle Park was an exceptionally busy one, being the main link between the South and points west, and Washington, D.C., New York, and other places farther up the East Coast—not to mention the traffic to and from the Park itself. "Diana sends her regards," Leon went on, glancing at the two other Visitors seated on either side of him.

"I'm sure she does," Chang said dryly. "I gather that you and I share the same degree of favor."

"More or less," Leon admitted. Chang's subtle sarcasm was not lost on him. Too valuable a zoologist to dismiss, he was sent here by Diana to get him out of her way. "Diana's affections are not noted for their extended duration," he went on. "I was guilty, I guess, of assuming otherwise."

"Neither is she noted for the clarity of her instructions," Freda, the Nordic-looking woman to his right, complained. "We were told only that you were to have breeding facilities and complete control within your own department. But what kind of facilities, Leon?" Freda, one of Chang's trusted aides, would be Leon's chief of staff.

"Sand," Leon said. "I was told that there are sand barrens in this part of the country."

"Farther toward the coast," Freda said, "but not right here in the Piedmont."

"Plenty of sand at Camp T-3," Chang said, "but if that's what you need, why weren't you assigned there?"

"I think Diana wants to keep this more or less secret," Leon said, "at least for a while. Even though Camp T-3 is not recognized for what it is by the humans, there's far too high a population near there, and the camp administrator has little patience for experimental work. He will be supplying me with breeding stock, however, if I can find a place to put it.''

"The camp isn't really suitable,'' Darin put in. He was a handsome man, apparently of Mediterranean descent. "Here we can make use of the facilities in the Research Triangle, both private industry and university. The scientists, faculty, and students don't need to know what they're working on in order for them to help us. Anything sensitive will stay with Leon and Freda.''

"But if there's no sand,'' Leon complained, "there won't be anything for anybody to work on.''

Chang looked at him speculatively. "Diana wouldn't be putting you into an impossible situation on purpose, would she?'' she asked with only a slight archness to her voice.

"She might,'' Freda said, "but why? If she wanted Leon discredited, she could do that without tricks. And that's not her way, you know that as well as I do.''

"Just a minute,'' Darin said, getting to his feet. He picked up the phone on Chang's desk and dialed an in-house number. "Send up that survey we made when we moved in,'' he told the person on the other end. "Should have remembered it before,'' he said to the others in the office, hanging up and resuming his seat. "There's a place not far from here that should suit Leon just fine.''

A moment later the office door opened and a clerk stepped in. Darin took the proffered folder and opened it on Chang's desk. Freda and Leon came to look at the map he displayed.

"Right here,'' Darin said, pointing. "An anomalous geological feature, twenty acres of sand surrounded by quartz rock formations on the north and east, and dense clay on the west and south. Totally worthless for farming, housing, or anything else. But perfect for Leon's project.''

"Looks good,'' Leon said. He pointed at some black dots near the indicated area. "Houses?''

"A large farmhouse, two barns, and several other buildings. They've been empty for quite awhile, but we can fix them up easily. I'll get hold of the county records tomorrow and have them deed the property over to us. We can start moving you in in the afternoon."

"Excellent," Leon said. He went back to his chair. "I needn't remind you," he went on, "that this project should not be discussed in front of those not actually involved."

"We understand that," Chang said softly. "Aside from your own staff, only the four of us will know anything about it."

"Good," Leon said. "I may not be in Diana's favor right now, but this could make a big difference in our control over this planet."

"If Lydia would just give me a little more leeway," Chang said, "I could control this part of the state without any trouble at all."

"That's as may be," Leon said, "but this is what we have to work with. If we're done here, maybe you can show me to a room, and I can let you get some rest."

"We get too much rest as it is," Chang complained. "Aside from a little student rebellion, nothing much happens here in this backwater."

"That's the last of them," Steve said, closing a panel he almost had to stand on tiptoe to reach.

"But we don't know what we're connected to," Mark complained.

"Well," Lester said, "we have some idea, and I've patched into all twelve outgoing phone lines, so we should be able to sort things out back at the lab."

"I sure hope so," Mark muttered. They packed up their tools and turned to the door where Anne was still waiting.

"All clear as far as I can tell," she said. She switched off the lights.

And they waited. Anne counted for them, and after five minutes their eyes were as adapted to the dark as they would ever be. Only then did she open the door to let them out into the dimly lit hall.

But as they worked their way back toward the stairs, they could hear voices, shouts, and thuds coming from one of the recreation rooms through which they had passed just an hour ago. Cautiously, Mark moved toward the noise and peered through a crack in a door.

"Looks like a goddamned judo lesson," he said when he came back. "That handball court—they've got mats out all over the floor."

"Can we use the stairs we were supposed to have come down by?" Anne asked Steve.

"Sure, but who knows where we'll wind up with the partitions all changed up there." He took out his plans again. "There's another stair at the far side," he said. "That's the east side of the building, where the kitchens are."

"Not likely to find any Visitors there," Mark said. "Okay, you lead the way."

They found the stairs with no difficulty, but the kitchen area was far from abandoned. Though the Visitors did not cook their food, they needed cage space for all the small animals they kept, and a butchery for the larger ones they fed on raw. And though it was now past three-thirty in the morning, there were still red-uniformed people about, apparently looking for snacks. Twice the four humans tried to pass through the area, and twice they were nearly discovered by one or more Visitors. Steve checked his plans over and over, but it looked as if that was the only way out.

"Let's try the front door," Anne suggested. "We'll have to circle the building, but if we don't get out soon, they'll find us in here, and then the whole game will be blown."

"Might as well try it," Mark agreed. "At least then we'll have a chance of escaping, even if we're discovered."

"Only one problem," Lester said. "Anne left tape on that door we came in by."

"Damn," Mark and Anne said together. "Okay," Mark said to Steve, "how can we get back there?"

"Just follow me," Steve said, folding up his map and putting it away.

*   *   *

After the tension of the tapping, and the anxiety of nearly being caught in the kitchen area, the ease with which they got back to the shipping department was anticlimactic.

But that, Mark knew, made the situation more dangerous than ever. High adrenaline had had no outlet, and overconfidence could make them careless. Indeed, as they left the building, Anne almost forgot to remove the tape which would have revealed their presence when the Visitors used the door the next day. And Mark himself forgot to wait until the guards had passed so that they were nearly caught as they crossed the parking area to the shelter of the ground vehicles.

"It all goes for nothing," he grated angrily to the others, "if we don't get away clean." Overhead, the sky was beginning to pale with the first light of morning.

After a forced pause to calm themselves, they started back north toward the woods. Moving from vehicle to vehicle, then from flyer to flyer, they got as far as the north end of the parking area when they had to wait once more for the guards to pass again.

"How many flyers were there before?" Lester asked.

"Four," Mark said. "Why?"

"There are five now," Lester said. "This one wasn't here when we went in."

"Damn." Mark looked back the way they had come and counted. "You're right," he said. "But they never keep more than four here, so that means—"

"That somebody could be coming out right now," Anne said, "to take this one away again."

"So let's move out," Mark said. "And if we're discovered, fight as though we're here on a raid and trying to get in instead of out."

"Good way to get ourselves killed," Steve said.

"That bug is more important than any of us," Mark reminded him. "Now go, but remember, don't dig up the lawn."

They crawled quickly, quietly, and carefully, across the gently sloping grounds back toward the fence. From here, a low crest concealed the gap they had made with the light pipes. When they got to the fence, they found themselves far to one side, and rather than crawl ran in a low crouch to the gap. Even as they did so they could hear the quiet rush and whine of the fifth flyer getting ready to lift.

"Down!" Anne called from behind, her voice just loud enough to be heard. They fell flat, dangerously near the bottom beam of the energy fence. Back at the parking area, the flyer lifted, straight up at first and then moving directly overhead. They froze in the dew-covered grass as the vehicle swung toward the west and away.

"Now move," Mark called over his shoulder, and again they scurried to the gap. "Easy through the fence," he admonished, "don't knock the light pipes away." Steve went through, bent nearly double. Lester followed him, and in his anxiety got his foot caught in one of the flexible hoses. He jerked, and the lens moved an inch, but did not fall out of the beam of the fence. Anne followed more carefully, and then they all crouched while Mark removed the three light pipes, one by one. He stowed one on each of their backs, and then they went on toward the trees, still low and not moving as fast as they wanted to. The sky overhead was growing brighter, and they were totally exposed instead of being cloaked in darkness.

Lester was the first one into the trees, with Steve and Anne close behind. Just as Mark made the shelter of the carefully tended forest they heard a sharp whistling siren screaming from the Visitor headquarters behind them.

There was no time for stealth. They ran. The upcoming dawn didn't help them under the trees, but they were able to keep together until they reached the untended area. But by that time the sounds of pursuit were growing louder behind them.

But at least the trees made it impossible for any flyers to see them. They ran an oblique course, not the way they had come but angling toward the east. As they ran, Mark pulled out a communicator and spoke into it between gasping breaths.

"We're hot," he said. "Make it point seven."

They crossed the shallow bed of the summer stream and paused to get their bearings on the other side.

"Did you get to Paul?" Anne asked as she drew her pistol and made sure the safety was off.

"I think so," Mark said. Steve and Lester, both panting heavily, were also making their weapons ready. They could hear the Visitors moving through the undergrowth on the other side of the shallow valley.

"Quietly but quickly," Mark said, his own gun out now. "Don't shoot unless you have to, but if you have to, make it clean."

They went up the gentle slope while behind them the Visitor guards got nearer. Dressed in dark green and black, the humans were all but invisible in the nightlike forest, while the Visitors, in their red uniforms, stood out as clearly as the British against the Minutemen. At last the humans came to the top of a rise and could hear, still half a mile away, the sounds of traffic on the north-south highway.

"Where's Paul taking the truck?" Steve asked, panting.

"The old furniture-stripping place," Mark said, pointing. "That way."

Just then a bolt of laser energy seared out from the trees off in the other direction, and Steve fell. Mark, Anne, and Lester dropped to their knees and opened fire. The scream that answered their shots was welcome, but now their position was known.

Mark and Anne grabbed Steve under the arms and started dragging him down the slope toward the highway and point seven, an agonizing half mile away. Lester, moving backward, kept low and covered their retreat. Small and pudgy, he was nobody's idea of a heroic soldier, but his shots were aimed with a frigid caution, and each one struck home. By the time Mark and Anne had Steve halfway to the highway, the pursuit had stopped to regroup. Only then did Lester turn to run after them.

More laser beams penetrated the dark morning air, but none found their mark. Again Lester took a post behind a

large tree, and kept the pursuers at bay while Mark and
Anne struggled with their burden. When he heard Anne call
to him, he wove a zigzag course through the trees, dodging
the aliens' fire. Twice shots came so close that he could feel
the static heat of their passage, and once he stepped into soft
ground that threw him headlong. He hit with a roll and was
on his feet, changing direction even as he did so.

Just a little way ahead he could see the truck, with only
Mark visible beside it. Paul, at the wheel, was starting to
move it southward—not north toward the rest of the Park
and Data Tronix—with Mark walking beside, in a half
crouch. Lester put on a burst, saw Mark take aim and fire,
and then he came out from the trees, running toward the
back of the truck. Inside, Anne reached out and took his
hand, boosting him inside while Mark piled into the
passenger's seat. Then with a squeal that shot gravel from
the shoulder high into the air and left black tire marks for a
hundred feet, the truck accelerated, cars behind it swerving
to avoid it, and they were away, leaving the red-uniformed
Visitors waving their weapons helplessly.

Chapter 2

Though it was June, there were still plenty of students on the University of North Carolina Chapel Hill campus for the summer session. Indeed, there were more students on the main quad now than at cooler times of the year. Here were three young men throwing two Frisbees, with a dog trying to make a fourth. There a couple lay on the grass under a huge water oak, oblivious to passersby. A group of sorority coeds ambled up one of the diagonal walks, planning their next party. Football players put in extra time so their course loads would be easier during the fall season.

To a casual observer, university life was unchanged from the days before the arrival of the Visitors. And that was just what made Peter Frye and his four companions less than pleased with the situation. They walked down the middle of the quad from Franklin Street toward the Old Well, watching their fellow students enjoying the fine summer weather.

"It's just too damn bad," Peter said. Though built like a football tackle, he was too short to play and had never cared much for the sport in the first place.

"My dad talks about the good old days in Berkeley," Benny Mounds agreed, walking beside him. As heavily built as Peter, Benny's weight was mostly fat. His agility was in his black fingers, not in his heavy arms and legs. As he walked, four half-dollars sparkled in the sun, weaving impossible figures in the air above his hand.

"You'd think nobody cared anymore," Greta Saroyan complained, on Peter's other side. She was tall and thin, and would have been pretty if she hadn't adopted a carefully grungy pseudo-farmer appearance.

"I don't think they do," Peter said. His other two friends, Dave Androvich and Edna Knight, followed behind within easy hearing distance. Peter looked over his shoulder at Dave. "Anybody in your dorm show *any* signs of life?"

"None," Dave said. He was so blond as to look almost like an albino, but his eyes were a deep brown. "All they care about is whether there's enough beer in the place."

"If we're going to shake these Visitors up," Edna said, "we'll have to do it ourselves." She was short, well-built, and obviously cared about her clothes, though she avoided anything that looked like a sorority style.

"That's just what I was thinking," Peter agreed.

They continued their discussion as they walked south between the brick and stone buildings, the old trees, the thick bushes. Occasionally they would see someone they knew and shout a friendly hello. Several other dogs wandered the quad as if they owned the place, and bicyclists whizzing past on the pavement made pedestrian life hazardous. That was why the five friends stuck to the grassy middle of the quad.

They paused at the Old Well to watch the traffic on Cameron Avenue. Across the street was South Building, and beyond that another quad. They all had time to kill before their next classes, and Peter didn't have any more until after lunch. But for the moment, classwork was the farthest thing from their minds. They could have avoided going this way, but like probing a canker sore, they had to do it. They crossed Cameron, went around South Building, and went down the middle of the south quad.

"I think it's time somebody did something about those lizards," Peter said. Everybody agreed, especially since, from here, they could see the Courtland Building halfway down the quad on the left, the place where the Visitors had their campus liaison offices.

"I'm tired of just talking about it," Edna complained, coming up to walk between Peter and Greta. "We should *do* something."

"That's just what I said," Peter told her. He was reluctant to allow anybody else to initiate ideas or actions. "You have something special in mind?"

Edna didn't answer.

"What we need," Benny said, "is somebody like Mike Donovan, somebody who's not afraid to stand up to the sonsa'bitches."

"What the hell has Donovan done lately?" Dave demanded. "Him and Julie Parrish have both been lying mighty low this last year or so."

"How do we know that?" Peter asked, trying to regain control of the conversation. "The Visitors practically control the networks. We wouldn't hear anything here even if Diana's Mother Ship fell on L.A."

"At least there's no Mother Ship over *our* heads," Greta said.

"That doesn't make me feel a hell of a lot better," Peter snapped. He stepped over the low wall in front of Wilson Library and onto the broad walkway at the foot of the steps.

"We ought to do something," Benny said. "But what?"

Durk Attweiler pulled his battered Ford truck into the last place in front of the Five Star Bar. It had been a long, hard day down at his farm, and he didn't feel like fixing himself supper. The Five Star was just across the county line, in Orange County, but it was nearer than the Estes Bar and Grill down in Churchill, and he liked the company here better. Down there, he had nobody to talk to except other farmers, most of whom were at least as badly off as he was, though for different reasons. Up here, with Chapel Hill just a few miles away, there were other types. No students or faculty ever came down this far into the country, thank God, but at least a guy got a chance to talk to some hard hats and other good old boys who did more than dig in the clay.

Walking into the bar was like walking from bright afternoon to late evening. Tom Rogers, the owner and bartender, kept the lights dim, but only partly as a matter of style. Visitors also came down here once in a while, just to lord it over the locals, though they didn't throw their weight around much. Still, Tom's wife made the best French dip sandwiches Durk had ever eaten, and the Visitors didn't intrude too often.

It was just late enough in the day that most of the people here had already had supper at home. Durk moved through the tables near the door to the end of the bar, and leaned on the dull wood surface, waiting for Tom to take care of another customer. The bar itself ran down the left side of the building, with booths opposite, while down the right was the eating area with tables and chairs. The end here was the cash register, and that's where Tom spent his time when he wasn't drawing at the taps.

Durk was a solid man, just under six feet tall, and built like a brick wall. His pale hair was thinning—he was nearly forty and that bothered him—but his hands were strong, his arms bulged through the sleeves of his shirt. His face was dark from the sun, bleached white above the line of his cap, which he now held in his hands. His mother had taught him to take his hat off indoors, and no amount of time in the Army, no number of sloppy old boys could make him not show at least that amount of respect.

"In kinda early, aren'tcha?" Tom asked, coming over at last. He put down a bottle of Stroh's and a frosty glass, knowing what Durk's first order would be.

"Got a taste for one of Elly's sandwiches," Durk said, pouring the beer carefully to minimize the head. "Couldn't stand my own cooking tonight."

"Coming right up. You want it here or at a table?"

"Table'd be fine," Durk said. He carried the glass and bottle over into the far corner of the eating area on the right and sat down, nodding at several acquaintances on the way. He sat, facing the entrance, watching the other people.

Most of them were men, laborers and a few farmers, janitors from the university and a couple of old boys who hadn't held a job in the last twenty years, as far as he could remember.

He slouched down in his chair and sipped his beer. The door beside his table opened and Wendel Fenister came out of the back, zipping his fly.

"Hey," Wendel said, "how you doing?"

"If it isn't clay," Durk said, "it's quartz, and if it isn't rocks, it's sand. If I had a mortgage on the place, they'd foreclose tomorrow."

"Goin' up to Pisgah in a couple weeks," Wendel said. "Drink a little shine, poach a little deer. Care to come along?"

"Love to, but no way. Gotta get the ditches clear before it rains again."

"If you change your mind, lemme know. Got room for one more in the van."

"I'll do that," Durk said. Wendel nodded and went on to join his other friends sitting at a table toward the front.

Durk took a long pull from his beer. He envied Wendel his freedom of movement. Fenister was always going hunting somewhere, and paid little attention to the fish and game laws. But, then, Wendel's farm was doing well; he had good land instead of the almost barren soil Durk had to contend with.

His reverie was broken by the sound of a familiar voice coming from the end of the bar. A moment later a huge black man, yellow hard hat perched on top of his head, came around the corner with a bottle and glass in one hand and a plate in the other.

"Yo, George," Durk called. George Monty saw him at once and came over.

"Here's your sandwich," George said, putting the plate down in front of Durk. "Tom's getting a little lazy." He pulled a chair out and sat down. George was one of the few men with whom Durk would tolerate that kind of familiarity.

"How's the highway?" Durk asked before taking a bite of the French dip.

"Got rocks in it, just like your farm," George answered. He poured his beer so the head overflowed and he had to bend over to slurp it off. "Broke the blade on a big dozer yesterday, hitting one of those boulders."

"Gonna make you pay for it?" Durk asked around a mouthful.

"Hell, no, I just dig where they tell me." He drank off half his beer and refilled his glass.

"Musta been a big rock."

" 'Bout the size of the dozer. Hell, man, what they want me to do? Had to get a dynamite crew in to blow it up. Ground's nearly as hard."

Durk felt comfortable with the big road worker. They both worked in dirt, though with different tools and toward different ends. Durk had known George Monty for nearly twelve years, and had liked the younger man from the start. It never occurred to him that he treated George differently from the other black "boys" he was polite to but ignored.

"Saw the damnedest thing this afternoon," Durk said after he'd finished his sandwich and allowed George to buy a pitcher to split. "I was cleaning ditches up at the northeast corner—"

"Know the place," George said. "Sand pits."

"Damn near enough sand to put in a beach if you had any water nearby. So there I am, the trencher going like crazy, least I get no beer cans up there like Murphy on the other side down by the county road. Anyway, I'm looking across the fence into the scrub and there's this deer."

"Goddamn," George said, and turned around to look where Wendel Fenister and his friends were sitting. "Wendel hear that? He'll be down on your place like a shot."

"Didn't tell him. Wouldn't do him any good anyway, because the deer's gone."

"You run 'm off?"

"Nope. Deer's about two hundred yards away, moving

around in the low bush, and all of a sudden it goes down. Didn't fall, it just sank. Fast. Threw its head up—four points, I reckon—and woulda yelled if it coulda. I got off the tractor and walked over to where it was, right by a scrawny pine no bigger'n a stick, and there's nothing there. Just a kinda hollow place in the sand."

"Quicksand?"

" 'At's what I figure, though how that could be with it being so dry and all I don't know. Didn't stick around. Figured I didn't wanna go down myself. Sure was strange, though."

Durk and George were into their third pitcher when the Five Star went quiet. George turned around so he could see the door.

Four Visitors, their red uniforms starkly out of place, stood near the end of the bar.

"Shit," George said—softly.

The Visitors spoke to Tom a moment, then came into the room. Two were women, one a tall Chinese, the other a very blond Nordic. The men were a black and an Italian or Greek. As they looked around, it was obvious they wanted a table to themselves. Several patrons accommodated them by getting up to move to other tables.

The lights, already low, were dimmed even further as the Visitors made their choice. Elly Rogers came out from the bar and cleaned off the table quickly and straightened the chairs for them. The Visitors sat, making themselves at home. People started talking again, but at a lower level than before.

Tom came out this time, with a large decanter of red wine and a cage of small animals. The Visitors accepted this, and even paid for it, as if such service was only to be expected. Which here, apparently, it was.

George turned back to Durk, so as not to stare. In truth, he didn't want to watch the Visitors eat their prey. Durk, half concealed behind the large man's body, couldn't keep his eyes off the four disguised aliens. The animals in the cage, he discovered, were just white rats, probably from the university, or maybe from the zoological testing center up at the Research Triangle Park. There were at least a dozen of the unfortunate creatures.

Watching the aliens eat did not disgust Durk, as it did many of the other patrons. He'd watched a black snake devour a rat and cheered the reptile on. After all, rats were a serious pest to a farmer, and black snakes and corn snakes were valued for eating them.

Rather, he got angry. The Visitors knew that most humans found their eating habits unpleasant. That they flaunted them here was a sign of their arrogance and condescension. The Visitors were enjoying their meal not for itself, but for the discomfort it caused the other patrons, a discomfort the patrons could do nothing about.

"I think I've had enough," George said. He wiped his mouth with a paper napkin.

"Eating rats ain't so bad," Durk said quietly, looking at his friend.

"My cat eats rats," George whispered intensely, leaning across the table toward Durk, "but not at my table, and not in my presence. I'm going home."

"Maybe a good idea," Durk said quietly. George got up, dropped a dollar on the table, and left. Durk watched him leave, and then began to realize what it meant to be made a nigger by those with the upper hand. He kept his eyes dutifully off the Visitors as he got up and walked toward the front door.

Data Tronix was one of the smaller computer science industries in the Research Triangle Park, and one of the most diverse in its products. They did not manufacture chips, but they designed them and the hardware to use them and the software to run them, specializing in data manipulation, transmission, and transformation.

Like all the companies in the Park, their building was set among carefully landscaped lawns and woods, occupying only five percent of the land they owned. It was invisible from the road, and not very prepossessing when one drove up the long driveway to the parking lot. It stood only two stories tall, starkly rectangular, unlike some of the others. But there were three floors underground, and service cellars below that.

On level A-1, the ground floor, were the reception area, the staff lounge, cafeteria, and public conference rooms. Administrative offices and special conference rooms occupied level A-2 above it. B-1, the first underground floor, was the domain of the software developers, B-2 was where the engineers worked, and B-3, airy and light in spite of being thirty feet underground, was the manufacturing facility.

Below that was C-1, which housed the physical plant—heating, cooling, power, and all necessary to the survival of the building. C-2, deep in the Carolina clay and gravel, was used only for long-term storage, one or two special silicon annealing furnaces, the high-power X-ray machines, and similar apparatus best kept out of sight, including one lab that had not been a part of the original design. Here, crowded into what had once been a storage room, were desk-top computers, a minimainframe, CRTs of all sizes and capabilities, and a new data line. All the CRT monitors were on, though most of them showed only garbage.

At one console sat Lester Ortega. Standing behind him were Mark Casey and a computer technician named Paul Freedman. Paul was in his fifties, weatherbeaten and gray but a man who took care of himself with plenty of exercise.

"Tapping the phone company was easy," Lester explained. They'd done that a week ago, just three days after their raid on the Visitor headquarters.

His terminal showed twelve windows, each with four lines of code. "Each of these," he went on, pointing at the screen, "is one of the lines coming out of Visitor headquarters. Ma Bell doesn't even know the signals are there. Not costing her anything, of course, since they aren't going anywhere but here."

"Looks like trash to me," Paul said. The twelve windows showed not only alphanumerics, but other odd symbols and graphic characters.

"It is, so far," Lester said. "That's what you and Bill and Shirley and I have to sort out." The other two, Bill Gray and Shirley Patchek, looked up on hearing their names.

"I'm going to run the splitter now," Bill said. He was a young black man, barely into his twenties, who'd been hired by Data Tronix when they'd discovered him using his personal computer to break into their personal data files three years ago. He was a sloppy worker but prone to fits of brilliance which more than compensated for that. He typed something in at his keyboard and twelve monitors around the room cleared, each one now showing one of the sets of code on Lester's monitor.

"Let's see if they're truly independent," Shirley said. She sat in front of one of the monitors and started typing. The image expanded to show a full twenty-four lines plus one status line. Nothing else changed.

"I told you it would work," Bill said. He'd designed the splitter program, but Shirley had done the actual writing and coding. Her perfectionism and lack of imagination complemented Bill's brilliance and eccentricity perfectly.

"Looks good," Mark said. "The first thing to do is to find out what each signal is."

"We've got several signals superimposed in each case," Lester said. "But I think we can write filters so that we can look at what we want."

"No problem," Bill said, "we'll just check the wave forms and run a statistical analysis." He flipped a switch and the top line on Lester's monitor went into reverse video at the same time that a separate monitor came to life, displaying a complicated wave pattern like an EKG readout.

"Just don't tell the people up in statistics what we're working on," Mark cautioned.

"Not to worry," Paul said. "As far as anybody upstairs knows, we're working on a subcontract from JPL to untangle the data from the *Galileo* probe."

"Is Anne covering that?" Mark asked.

"She's even got letters from Kline and Bergholm to that effect," Paul said. "In fact, given thirty seconds' warning, we can even switch to real *Galileo* tapes."

"And," Lester said, "unless the Visitors can trace the signals from their main buses through the phone lines to us, which even Ma Bell can't do, there's no way they can know we're involved at all."

"Sounds like you've got it knocked," Mark said as the one phone rang on a table in the middle of the room. He reached for it, listened a moment, and then hung up.

"Steve's going to be all right," he said, and a certain extraneous amount of tension went out of the room. "That was Memorial," naming the huge teaching hospital in Chapel Hill. "Steve's out of critical condition, and he's going to hurt when he laughs, but he'll be back on the job in a couple days."

"Damn," Lester said, and leaned his head in his hand with relief.

"All right then," Mark said. "I'll leave you people to it. Just a minor miracle, that's all I'm asking."

"We've done 'm before," Paul said. Mark nodded and left them to their jobs.

The three were a team and got results very quickly. Paul could understand signals, knew information theory, and had a knack for distinguishing garbage from useful data. Bill, taking Paul's suggestions, figured out ways to implement them, while Shirley, who wrote assembly language in her sleep, worked up the programs to do what Bill suggested to achieve what Paul wanted.

But it was not a trivial problem. They were more than satisfied when, after four hours, they knew which of the signals were just fluctuations in power lines, which were telephone lines, both internal and external, and which were other signals including the Visitors' many computers.

It was the phone lines that Bill and Shirley were most interested in. Their plan was to separate the external calls from the in-house numbers, and convert the analogue signals into sounds so they could eavesdrop on anything any Visitor said to anybody else, either at their headquarters or elsewhere. But Paul kept looking at the filtered-out power signals.

"They aren't using a steady draw," Paul said, interrupting the other two in the midst of an argument. "And if what you've done to separate the lines has any meaning, then I think we can do something with that."

"Like what?" Bill wanted to know.

"Like figuring out not only how much power they use, but by comparing different lines and doing a separation analysis, what power is being used in what part of the building."

"So, lights?" Bill said. "Air conditioning? What difference does it make?"

"Those are constant. But look." He pointed at a large monitor which combined several power signals into one display, each with a different color. "If we take out those constants, what we have left can only be special equipment. If we can tell when they're using the kitchen, the upstairs offices, and so on, we can discount those too, and know when they're using sound detectors or anything else that draws only on demand. Some things won't make any sense one way or another, but they've got some equipment in there and if we can find out what's where, by eavesdropping on their in-house orders and so on, we could learn a lot about what they're doing."

"I've gotcha," Bill said. "They've got a conversion machine in there, and we could sort of peek in on them when they use it. But first we'd have to know where it is, and that means the phone lines have to be figured out."

"So let's do it," Shirley said. "Once we've got those separated, you can hear them in person."

"Well," Paul hesitated, "nearly."

"Bullshit," Shirley said, "I'll reconstruct their voices exactly. All we need is a good speaker system, and I'll get the stockroom to supply us with one tomorrow. But we've got twelve outgoing lines, and God knows how many internal ones. Let's get on it."

Those who would throw off the yoke of oppression know no time clocks. It was in the not so small hours of the next morning that Paul Freedman, Bill Gray, and Shirley Patchek finally quit. In that time they had managed to identify seventeen major internal power lines at the Visitor headquarters, eleven computer complexes, and sixteen intercom systems, apart from the twelve outside phone lines.

Shirley had not waited to get speaker systems for the voice communications, but had gone up to supply on B-3 and purloined what she had needed. While they had worked on other problems, they had eavesdropped on several conversations, most of them meaningless, and recorded every one for later analysis. Under Paul's supervision, and with Bill's somewhat erratic insight, Shirley had written assembly code on the spot, transforming complex signals into comprehensible dialogue. Comprehensible, at least, in the sense that what came out of the speakers were words. What the words meant or might imply was something else.

But that was for Mark and Anne to worry about. Shirley's main concern was to figure out the computer signals. With eleven different computers at the Visitor headquarters, each in communication with the others and some of them connected to the outside lines, there was a lot of data to sort through just in determining which signal originated with which computer, let alone what those signals meant.

And that, of course, was what they were really after. When she could no longer think in assembly language, Shirley decided to call it a day—or a morning, rather. The three left their secret lab, with the satisfaction of knowing that they at last had an inside line to the Visitors' activities.

* * *

Peter Frye met Benny Mounds and Edna Knight on the steps of Hanes Hall, across the quad from the Visitor office in the Courtland Building. It was nearly lunchtime, and hundreds of students were walking from classes back to dorms or up to Franklin Street.

"Where's Greta and Dave?" Peter asked his friends.

"Haven't seen Dave," Edna said. "Greta's doing her laundry. She'll be here as soon as she can."

"Great, just great," Peter said. "We're trying to get these damned lizards off our backs, and Greta's got to do laundry. Maybe I should go home and shine my shoes."

"Come on, Peter," Benny said. "We can tell her about it later."

"You can bet that Mike Donovan and Julie Parrish didn't postpone any planning sessions to do laundry," Peter returned. He knew he was sounding foolish, but Greta's absence made it all too clear that he didn't have the kind of control over his fellows that he would have liked.

"I suppose we could just sit here and wait," Edna said sarcastically. "And I don't see why we can't talk in our rooms or down in the student union."

"Because it's not safe," Benny said. "The lizards have bugs planted in some of the rooms, and I know they've got cameras at the union."

"They can't have bugs in *all* the dorm rooms," Edna protested.

"Maybe not, but do you want to take the chance? Out here in the open is the best place to talk."

"So let's talk, then. What are we going to do?"

"We can start," Peter said, "by finding all the bugs we can and ripping them out."

"Hell," Benny said, "I do that anyway, and the lizards just put them back."

"Seems like it would be easier," Edna suggested, "if we could destroy their listening post instead."

"I think you've got a good idea," Peter said. "That would put all their bugs out of commission at a single whack."

"It would take them at least a couple days to fix it," Benny added.

"More likely they'd bring in new equipment overnight," Peter went on. "But look, you know they've got to have a lot of records in there." He looked past Edna at the Courtland Building across the quad. A Visitor in red had just come out and was going up toward Cameron Avenue.

"And destroyed records," Edna said, following his gaze, "can't be repaired or replaced."

"At least not easily. I wonder how much damage we could do with a pair of wire cutters and a hammer."

"Enough to neutralize the lizards for a couple of weeks at least," Edna said. "And I'll bet we could get other people to help us after we show them it can be done."

"Now we're talking," Peter said happily. "Trashing the lizards' office will be just the first step. Once we get some people organized, we'll be able to make those lizards wish they'd never heard of Chapel Hill."

"Question is," Edna said, "how are we going to get into the building?"

"No problem," Benny told her. He held up his hands and wiggled his thick brown fingers at her. "My dad's a locksmith, and he taught me all he knows."

"Terrific," Peter said. "And I think we ought to move quickly."

"Like when?" Edna asked. "Tonight?"

"Sure, why not? Get a few tools you can carry easily. We'll meet here at three."

"In the morning?"

"Unless you want to do it this afternoon. And when you see Greta, tell her laundry's no excuse this time."

The ancient ditcher hooked up to the three-point hitch of the tractor strained and clanked as Durk Attweiler guided it along the fence line at the southeast corner of his farm. Heavy, sandy clay spewed erratically from the top end of the scoop chain into the wagon towed behind. It was four in the afternoon, and the wagon would be filled by the time he got to the road at the south, in another half hour or so, and he would quit then. Ditching was not his favorite activity, but if he didn't do it, his fields would be waterlogged in spring and fall, and he wouldn't be able to either plant or harvest his sparse crops.

The next farm east, across the fence line, had long since been allowed to return to forest. The trees, mostly loblolly pine, were spindly and weak. Old man Thurston, without heirs, had just quit working the place when he'd turned seventy, and not even the state had wanted the property when he'd died two years ago at eighty-three.

As he chugged along, Durk passed the end of the forest and could now see Thruston's weathered gray farmhouse up on the hill, just a half mile away. The soil was different there, and instead of pines, the one-time cornfield was spotted with cedar trees, none of them more than ten feet tall and most less than five.

He heard a car down on the highway, but instead of going by, it turned up Thurston's drive. Durk could just barely see it as it passed behind the cedars, a big black car of a make he didn't recognize. It stopped at the house, and several people got out. The cedars were between him and them, so he couldn't see who they were, but as they went up onto the porch, he saw a flash of red just before they went into the house. A moment later somebody came out and drove the car around to the far side of the house and out of sight.

Who would want to buy that farm? he wondered as he struggled to keep the ditcher on course. If there was any farm in Churchill County that was poorer than Durk's it was the Thurston place. Where there wasn't clay, there was quartz rock, and where there wasn't quartz, there was nearly sterile sand. The only reason Thurston had been able to keep the place going was because his grandfather had found gold in the quartz a century ago, and though the gold had run out quickly, the elder Thurston had left just enough money to make ends meet.

At last Durk reached the ditch that ran along beside the highway. That was somebody else's worry, not his. He disengaged the ditching mechanism and raised the lower end of the scoop chain clear of the ground. It would be five by the time he got back to the house, and he was ready for a hot shower and a cold beer.

He sat for a moment on his tractor, letting the engine idle, looking back over his shoulder at Thurston's house. Maybe the people who had bought the place were looking to do some tree farming instead of planting crops. He thought he might walk up to the place, say hello, introduce himself, find out who they were and what they were up to.

But just as he reached down to turn off the tractor's engine, a movement in the sky up to the north and east caught his eye. It was an alien skyfighter, heading right this way. They passed over every now and then, going south from the Research Triangle Park to someplace toward Fayetteville, but usually their route was farther east. This skyfighter was heading right toward him. For a panicky moment he wished he had his shotgun.

He sat and watched as the craft grew nearer and then descended to land behind the Thurston house. He remembered the flash of red he'd seen when the people in the car had gone up onto the porch. Damned if he wasn't going to have a bunch of lizards for neighbors. It would not, of course, be a good idea to go calling on them.

But, he wondered, what the hell would Visitors be doing in a run-down place like this?

It was Durk's usual practice to dump his ditch dirt into the Saksapaw River, which formed the western boundary of his farm. The river was fairly deep and swift, and his little dirt didn't hurt it any, though most everybody else used a landfill a couple of miles east of his place. Today, he thought, maybe he'd do it that way, though it would take him an hour or so longer to finish the job. It would also take him right by the Thurston house, which was only a couple hundred feet from the road. He wanted to get a closer look at that skyfighter.

He got off his tractor, disconnected the ditcher, and hitched the wagon in its place. He couldn't get onto the highway here because the road ditch was too deep, but there was a crossing a little ways away where he'd laid tile just so he could get out if he wanted to—like now. He drove there, the heavily laden wagon leaving deep tire marks in the dry soil, crossed the ditch to the other side of the highway, then started toward the landfill.

Normally he hated to move so slowly on a road. There was no shoulder here, and the one or two cars that came up behind him had to pass by swinging way out into the other lane. But this time he didn't push it. Indeed, he kept the tractor at a creeping ten miles an hour. It took him awhile to come abreast of the Thurston house, but it also gave him plenty of time to see who and what was up there.

There were at least half a dozen Visitors moving around, going from the house to their big car and back, carrying boxes and things. The skyfighter was parked at the far side, between the house and a barn, and other Visitors were unloading it. He couldn't tell what any of the stuff was. He watched the house and his new neighbors with open curiosity as he drove slowly past, noticed that the windows were all opaqued somehow, and that something was being done to the inside of both the near and far barns without changing their external appearance.

Two of the Visitors were standing at the front end of the skyfighter, talking to each other and directing the work of the others. When they turned around to watch him drive past, it was all he could do to return their stare, and then turn slowly away. They were two of the lizards who had come into the Five Star last night, the tall black man and the Chinese woman. He didn't know whether they recognized him or not, but the thought that they might sent shivers up his spine.

He kept his eyes rigidly on the road after that. He had an

urge to dump the dirt and then come back another way so as not to pass in front of the house again, but if the lizards were watching him, that would be suspicious. As it was, he had every reason to be going where he was going. And coming back with an empty wagon, he would be able to crank the tractor up to twenty. The less time he spent under their observation, the better.

"This place is going to work out just fine," Leon told Chang as they walked past the skyfighter toward the barns at the back of the house. "Plenty of room, the structures are sound, and Freda tells me the sandy area north of here is large enough for ten or more animals in a nearly natural state."

"How's the one doing that you brought with you?" Chang asked. They entered one of the barns, which was being converted into a shop and garage.

"Just fine. A really superb specimen." They looked around at the work being done.

The walls of the barn had been lined with a plasticlike sheathing, onto which shelves were being fitted. Workbenches lined the back wall, and a heavy-duty rack was being installed to one side. In the middle of the floor were two strange vehicles. Each had an open cab at one end with two seats, but the rest was just a flat bed, supported on three-foot-tall balloon tires, like those used on a dune buggy, only larger.

"We'll be making cages in here," Leon said. "Won't need many big ones, of course, but the smaller animals can't be let loose, so we'll be keeping them in the other barn beside the house."

"About how many are you planning to have?" Chang asked.

"A hundred breeding pairs. Let's go take a look."

They left the garage and shop and walked up the other side of the skyfighter to the larger barn. It too had been sheathed, and several workers were installing racks from which the cages would be suspended along three walls and in a double row up the middle. A prototype cage was standing on the floor. It was two feet high, four feet wide, and eight feet deep, with a movable divider down the middle. The bottom was suspended over a clean-out tray, and there were food and water dispensers at the sides.

"The females will all go into the right side," Leon explained, "and we'll provide nesting material, of course. The divider keeps the male away from the female and pups during the first few days after birth."

"When do you expect your stock?" Chang asked.

"Tomorrow morning. We'll also be bringing some animals up from Camp T-3 then too. We could have brought them up today—they have plenty down there—but Freda wanted to make sure the grounds were secure."

They looked around a moment longer, and then went into the house.

Most of the Visitors there were workers and, like those in the shop and breeding barn, would depart when their week-long jobs were done, late that night or early the next day. But three would be staying on with Leon, as his staff. These three—Vivian, a white woman; Edmond, who looked like a Chicano; and Gerald, a white man—were directing the workers in their unloading and arranging of furniture and equipment.

Here too the entire inner surface had been refinished with the plasticlike sheathing, only, in this case, it was surfaced to look more like an office or residence instead of being left raw as in the shop and barn. The major portion of the first floor was being converted into a series of labs. The living room held surgical tables—two small ones and one large one—with all the adjunct equipment against the walls. The parlor held cages like those in the barn, but more compact, more elaborate, and with electronic equipment stacked around them. What had been the dining room now contained the top of a cage which extended through the floor and the crawl space below into a sand-filled pit. Only the kitchen retained its original function, although it was modified now to accommodate the Visitors' special culinary requirements.

After this brief tour, Leon and Chang went upstairs. The master bedroom had been converted to an office, where Darin was now supervising the installation of communications equipment and computers. The rest of the second floor had been modified into five small bedrooms for Leon and his staff.

"Not exactly spacious," Chang commented.

"They'll serve," Leon said. "We're going to be pretty busy once the animals get here, and there's plenty of room outside if people want some recreation."

"As long as they stay clear of the sand pits," Chang commented dryly.

They were about to depart when Freda came up the stairs, carrying what looked like an oversized leather folder.

"I've got the survey here," she told Leon. "Want to look at it?"

"Sure." He made space on one of the desks in the office, where Freda put down her folder and opened it. The inner faces were a translucent white, with a row of icons printed down one side. She touched one of these and a digitized aerial photo of the farm filled one half of the folder.

"Here's the house," she said, pointing. "And here's the sand pits." She touched another icon, and that part of the image enlarged, filling the flat screen. The screen on the other half of the folder now showed a list of terms in the alien script, each adjacent to a patterned square.

"Clay all down here," Freda went on. The pattern at the edge of the sand pits matched the term "clay" on the other screen. "Quartz rock outcropping over there, and projecting a bit into the sand. Most of the sand, as you can see, is white alluvial, but some, up in these areas, is like a porous fine red gravel. The important thing is that the clay and/or rock surrounds the sand area completely, though there is some mixing over here." She pointed to an area that corresponded to Durk Attweiler's north acreage. "It's shallow, however, and not at all suitable for the animals, and even if they do get there, the clay gets dense again." She touched a few more icons, the image enlarged, than shrank, and she showed them different portions of the range.

"I think it's really going to work," she said at last, turning off the display and closing the folder.

"It certainly looks like it," Leon said. "And if it does, Diana may look more favorably on us again."

"That would be very pleasant indeed," Chang said.

Chapter 3

There were no windows in the secret lab deep beneath Data Tronix. Paul Freedman turned from one screen, on which an overlapping series of sine waves recorded power usages at the Visitor headquarters, and went over to where Steve Wong sat stiffly at another monitor showing snapshots of a computer program in progress. Shirley Patchek stood beside Steve—it was her program that was running.

"That's it," Steve said. His breathing was shallow because of the tight bandages he wore around his chest, covering the wound he'd received over a week ago. "It should run now."

He rekeyed the computer, and on a larger display a graphic image of the first-floor plan of the Visitor headquarters came on. Shirley reached down beside the lower monitor and picked up a phone handset.

"We're on, Mark," she said into it.

"And we're set here." Mark's amplified voice came from the speaker set in the wall so that they all could hear.

"What lights are on?" Shirley asked. Mark answered with a string of numbers corresponding to windows on the plan display. Steve entered these at the keyboard, making those windows stand out in highlight. He touched another key and the second-floor display came on.

"Second floor," Shirley said into the phone. Mark responded with another string of numbers. More windows, all on the north side, were highlighted. There weren't very many of these, but that was what they wanted. If all the lights were lit, the power-draw-analysis program would have told them nothing.

"How about you, Anne?" Shirley asked.

"First floor, east side," Anne answered, and like Mark, repeated a series of numbers. While she was speaking, Mark was moving around to the west side. Then it was his turn to report again while Anne moved to the south side. It was their fifth cycle around the building in as many days. When all the windows were reported, Shirley told them to come on home.

A second large graphics display showed a tentative circuit plan, based largely on the construction plans, and modified according to what data they had been able to dig out of the power-draw signals they'd been receiving ever since they'd separated them from other signals of various kinds. Many of these circuits were now confirmed by Mark and Anne's reports, but others were still in doubt.

"From the lights they saw," Steve was saying, "we can assume that there is a partition here, since this window was lit and the one next to it was dark." He used a graphics program to draw in the new wall. "Same here and here. Now, they might have taken down a wall here, but we can't tell that." He indicated the wall with a question mark.

"That means that these circuits," Paul said, looking at yet another display, "are all lighting and similar household uses, while these"—as his fingers touched the keys, circuit lines changed from white to green—"are probably used for other things. They're all higher than one-ten."

Most of the screens showed plans or diagrams of one sort or another. They had, by this time, identified all internal phone lines, but didn't yet know to which rooms or phones they led. That was one of the things they hoped to learn tonight, at the conclusion of Mark and Anne's dangerous observations. If a phone was in use, it would be in one of the lit rooms rather than in a darkened one.

They had also been able to correlate Mark and Anne's observations with certain other high-power usages. In one case, a light had gone on, there'd been a brief massive power draw, which had stopped just before the light had gone off. From other data, they knew that that power had been used for the simple conversion equipment the Visitors had here and thus they'd been able to locate it exactly.

Slowly, piece by piece, their knowledge of the interior of the Visitors' headquarters was building up. During the day, they'd monitored every in-house and out-going phone conversation. Many of these were in the aliens' own language, and could not as yet be translated, but most were in English. All such conversations had been recorded, and those which contained any information or clues about the layout of the headquarters had been studied to help flesh out the picture.

"I think they've got their main computers over here," Steve said, pointing to a room on the second-floor display. "We know this power line"—he pointed to the other screen—"goes there, and it fluctuates in a way that reminds me of disk drives going on and off."

"I don't think they use disk drives," Paul objected.

"Maybe not, but that's what it feels like."

"What *I* want to know," Shirley said, "is where's their main communications center?"

"It's got to be one of these three places," Steve answered. "They all show a constant drain. But we're going to need to fine-tune the carrier-signal analyzer, and we'll need some observations of people actually using phones."

"We'll have to do that another night," Paul said. "I hate to have Anne and Mark out there in danger, but with their observations, we've been able to learn a lot."

"We're going to need to learn a lot more," Shirley said, "but I'm too tired to think right now. When are Bill and Lester coming down?"

"They take over in about fifteen minutes," Paul answered. "Maybe Bill will come up with some bright ideas."

"Anything's fine with me," Steve said, leaning back in his chair and stretching carefully, "as long as they're not late getting down here. I need about two beers and about twelve hours' sleep.''

"I'm with you on that one," Shirley said as they started preparing to change shifts.

Peter Frye's favorite tool was a two-foot-long screwdriver. It was lighter than a crowbar, and handier, and with it he had been able to open every filing cabinet in the Courtland Building office. Dave Androvich had wanted to burn all the papers they'd removed, but both Peter and Greta Saroyan had pointed out that that would have set off the sprinklers and brought the fire department. Edna Knight thought that one of the alien machines might be a shredder, but they couldn't identify it and so had compromised by ripping the documents up and soaking them with strong bleach in a big sink in the janitor's closet down the hall. The resulting mess was more than adequately useless.

Dave had preferred a hammer. With it he broke every terminal screen, pounded in every meter and gauge, and smashed whatever else would smash. At first they worried about the noise, but Benny Mounds had gone out into the hall to listen and came back reporting that as far as he could tell the whole office complex was soundproof. Dave went at it with enthusiasm. Even telephones did not escape his destructive energies.

Greta had been able to bring in a big pair of wire cutters, the handles nearly three feet long. No cable, wire, or conduit was spared. She cut connectors off short both at the devices and at the wall, and then cut the cables and wires into smaller sections. The cutters were strong enough that she could even use them to snip the knobs off the interior doors, though occasionally Peter or Dave had to give her a hand.

Edna occupied herself with the contents of the desks. Occasionally Peter would have to pry a drawer open for her, but once in she sorted through everything quickly. Office supplies just went into a wastebasket. Any papers that looked meaningful she shredded and added to Peter's collection in the janitor's sink. There were other things that she didn't recognize, and these she put out on top of the desks for Dave to smash, if he could.

Benny was the only one who didn't actively participate— at least at first. After letting them into the building, he had followed them up to the offices and just stalked from room to room, watching the destruction, but visibly growing tenser with every passing moment. Several times the others chided him for not joining in, but he just grimaced, shook his head, and wandered off to watch someone else work.

His turn came when they were almost finished. He took a big spray can with an industrial label out of the paper bag he'd been carrying, and started spraying a colorless fluid on every surface that someone might touch.

"Keep your hands off this," he cautioned. "It's glue. Very strong, but it takes twenty-four hours to dry." He sprayed slashed chair backs, desk tops, those doorknobs Greta hadn't been able to cut off, doorjambs, cabinet handles, and on and on. He emptied six of the cans before he was finished.

"That ought to hold them for a while," he said.

"We'd better get moving," Peter said, glancing at his watch. "It's five-thirty, and the custodians will be here in half an hour."

They left the office complex, closing the outer door carefully behind them, and went down the hall to the stairs of the first floor. The place was silent, and there were no signs of any early visitors—or Visitors.

They went to the double glass doors at the front, and while the others remained back a ways in the shadows, Benny went to see if anybody was in the quad. Dew sparkled in the morning light outside. He pushed against the bar to open the door but it wouldn't open.

"What's the matter?" Peter asked, coming up.

"I don't know," Benny said, pushing harder. "It opened easily enough when we came in."

"So pick the lock again."

"I can't. The keyhole is on the outside."

"Maybe it's just jammed," Edna said. "Let's go around to the side door."

They went, but the solid wood door there wouldn't open either. Benny tried his lock picks, but by now he was flustered and could make no headway.

"There's got to be a fire door in the back," Dave suggested. And indeed there was, a double metal door with emergency bars. But when Benny and Peter pressed, the bars swung without resistance and the doors stayed closed.

"What the hell is going on?" Greta cried.

"I don't know," Benny yelled, kicking at the immovable panels. "Fire doors are *always* supposed to open from the inside. *All* these doors are supposed to open from the inside."

"So we'll go out a window," Dave said, swinging his hammer. "Which side is closer to the ground?"

"The sills are all about eight feet up," Peter said. "Let's go to the basement."

They found the stairs down, but all the offices and storerooms down there were locked. Peter used his screwdriver to pry the lock off one, and they went in. It was a copying room, with Xerox and 3M machines, and a table which they pushed up to a window. But the glass there was wire impregnated, and Dave's blows just starred the glass without breaking it away.

"Quiet," Edna hissed. They all fell silent. Upstairs they could hear footsteps, several sets of them, moving around.

"Shit," Peter said. "Damn janitors."

"At least one of the doors is now open," Benny said. "Look, I'll go up, you follow. I'll distract the guy and we'll go out."

"They'll know who we are," Edna protested.

"They'll know who *I* am," Benny said. "I'll make a sudden trip back home, and lie low for a while."

"You're a hero, Benny," Peter said with obvious admiration.

With the other four following at a distance, Benny Mounds left the copy room and went up the stairs to the first floor. But it wasn't a janitor who stood a short way down the hall with a gun drawn. It was a red-uniformed Visitor. Benny's stomach knotted, and he raised his hands.

"What's happening?" Peter whispered up at him. He could see Benny but nobody else.

"The game's up," the distinctive resonant voice of the alien answered him. "Everybody come up nice and easy."

"I can't believe it," Greta whispered, watching as Benny moved out of sight to be replaced by two armed Visitors who stood at the top of the stairs, smiling down at them with drawn weapons.

"Come along," one of the Visitors, a woman, said. "You've had your fun."

Peter, Greta, Edna, and Dave all raised their hands helplessly. "At least," Peter said, "you won't be using that office for a while."

"We don't need to," the male Visitor said, smiling. "That was just the public office. The real one is on the floor above."

Durk Attweiler drove his truck up Old Pittsboro Road from the bypass into Chapel Hill. It was a quarter to seven, and he wanted to get his business done at the FCX when they opened so he could get back to work ditching. It was still too early for much traffic, so he had no difficulty going by the campus, until he got to the corner of Columbia and Cameron. There, a large, all-white Visitor truck of some kind stood at the corner, with red-uniformed guards all around. One by one the cars ahead of him were stopped, the drivers questioned, and then sent on.

As he waited his turn, wondering what the hell was up at this hour of the morning, he noticed another group of guards escorting four—no, five students, three boys and two girls, up to the waiting truck. One by one they were shoved inside.

The next car was let go, then the next, and now it was Durk's turn, but the procedure halted while the alien paddywagon pulled away from the corner and started up Columbia toward Franklin Street. Damn fools, Durk said to himself. Kids ought to know better than to cause trouble with the lizards right on their campus.

The guard signaled him to come forward. He stopped by the alien man, rolled down his window, and without waiting to be asked, took out his wallet and showed his driver's license.

"What's your business?" the guard asked.

"Going to the Farmers' Central Exchange for some medicine for my goats," Durk answered.

"Move along."

Durk did not roll his window up until he was well past the intersection.

He turned left onto Rosemary, took the right fork at Weaver, then right again up Greensboro to the FCX. Though it was still before seven, there were already several cars parked beside the long building. He pulled into a place and got out to join the four other men, none of them farmers, who were waiting for the Exchange to open.

At last Wilma Southerland, who'd been clerking there since Durk could remember, came to unlock the door and they all went inside. Durk went right to the medical shelves. He had a pretty good idea what was ailing his goats, but he read the lables on the inoculation kits just the same. Then he checked the prices. Like everything, the cost had gone up. He counted his money. If he drank his own moonshine instead of a couple of six-packs, he could buy three kits instead of two. Maybe two would be enough. He could come back for more later if he needed it.

Wilma was busy at the moment, answering questions about squash bugs. The man wore a suit, so he was probably one of the faculty doing a little shopping before his first class.

"That reminds me," the man said for no apparent reason. "New gloves."

"Just leave your things here, Professor Barnes," Wilma said, putting his purchases to one side of the counter. The man went off.

Durk went up and put down his two inoculation kits.

"How you doing, Durk?" Wilma asked.

"I'm okay, but the goats aren't," Durk answered. Wilma rang up the sale, and took the Exchange card he offered. The rebate at the end of the year wouldn't be much, but every little bit helped.

"Hope they all pull through," Wilma said, putting the kits into a bag.

"Hey, Morton," someone called out. Durk turned to see another faculty type addressing Professor Barnes. "We just had a bust on campus." The six or so other customers now in the store stopped to listen.

"What happened?" Barnes asked.

"As far as I can tell," the other man said, "several students trashed the Visitor Campus Liaison offices in Courtland. Got caught, of course."

"Damn fools," Barnes said, coming back to the counter with a pair of women's garden gloves. "Who were they?"

"I don't know," the other man said. "I wasn't there when they were taken away; that's just what I heard when I came by on my way here. Six of them, I think."

"Five," Durk said. "Three boys and two girls. One of the guys was black, and one of the girls was very tall."

"You saw them?"

"They had a guard checking IDs. Five kids got loaded into a truck and driven off."

"The only way we'll know who they are," Barnes's friend said, "is when they don't show up for classes."

"What's going to happen to them?" Durk asked.

"Prison camp," Professor Barnes answered. "No trial, of course."

"For how long?" Durk asked.

"For as long as the lizards want them," Barnes said bitterly. "Not very many people get out once they're in. A student of mine got picked up last semester, but his family had some kind of pull with the Visitors and he was released after only three months. Mostly you never see them again."

"Where is he now?" the other man asked.

"Back in Colorado. The red toxin is still effective up there most of the year. I don't blame him. One trip to that camp would be more than enough for me."

"Do they beat them?" Wilma asked.

"No, just make them work. I gather from the letter he sent me that life there isn't really very bad, especially when compared to our own prison system. But they have some kind of weird creature guarding the place. Lives in a sand-filled moat just outside the fence. Kenny saw a guy try to make a break for it once. The guards just watched as this guy climbed the fence and started running across the sand. Then all of a sudden these things like big snakes came up out of the sand and dragged him down into it. After that, Kenny decided, if he got out, which he did two weeks later, he'd just stay clear of the Visitors for the rest of his life."

Durk reached out and took his purchases off the counter. He pushed past the two men, who stared at him in surprise at his rudeness. But all Durk could think of was the deer he'd seen being sucked down into the sand.

The communicator on Chang's desk beeped. The RTP Area Administrator put down the report she was reading and touched the on button.

"This is Timothy over at UNC Security," the resonant voice said from the speaker. "We've got five students in custody." He narrated briefly what Peter Frye and his friends had done.

"They didn't even know about the third-floor offices?" Chang asked when he'd finished.

"Never guessed. I think it really spoiled their day when we told them."

"Well, at least no permanent damage has been done. Was anybody hurt?"

"Not at all. And I think we've got some good brain potential here. Their destruction was quite imaginative, and they're all A or B students."

"Good. Send them down to Camp T-3. Have Donald put them through a full set of suitability tests as soon as possible. Those we can convert, we will. The others, well, we'll work them till they're fat enough."

"One of them already is," Timothy said with a dry chuckle, and signed off.

Mark Casey and Anne Marino were down in the secret lab below Data Tronix. They were exhausted by their night's activity scouting the Visitor headquarters to the south, as well as having to put in regular time at work upstairs as well, but they wanted to see the fruits of their efforts firsthand.

They stood on either side of Shirley Patchek as she worked at a table, assembling a large-scale map of the Visitor headquarters. Paul Freedman brought over another printout. This was a high-resolution screen dump of a portion of the plan, which Shirley would trim to fit in with the others already assembled. Each sheet, measuring eight-by-ten inches, showed an area about forty-by-sixty feet. As new data came in, or changes were made to the image stored in the computer, Paul would print out a new sheet to replace an outdated one.

"We still can't figure out what they did in that area where they put up all the new partitions in the stock department," Shirley was saying. "Most of those rooms are interior with no windows. But there is some heavy equipment there, and at least one computer."

"You're doing a great job," Anne said, straightening up from the table. She turned to Paul. "Any progress on those internal messages?" she asked.

"Most of them are just typical office communication," he

said, going over to a terminal where he called up a data file. "At least, as far as we can tell. Those that refer to specific projects seem to fall into three main classes—general administration and security"—he punched a button and a menu appeared on the screen—"reports monitoring the companies here in the Park," he moved the cursor to an entry labeled "Misc," "and communications with liaison officers at the universities around the area." He pushed a button and the menu was replaced with a new one. "And then," he went on, "there are these here that don't seem to fall into any category." He sat back so Anne, and Mark too, could read over his shoulder.

"Who's 'Leon'?" Mark asked, reading the first of seven items in the menu.

"Somebody in charge of a special project. Not everything in his file has to do with that. Some of it is reports back to Diana—or Lydia—in the Los Angeles Mother Ship. Other items are personal communications with no significant content. But others refer to things listed in the other six files."

"That doesn't look like computer or communications subjects," Anne said. "I thought that was all the lizards were doing here."

"So did I," Paul said. "Ironic, Durham is the City of Medicine, but the Visitors do nothing but electronics. Except for this."

"'Sand Barrens,'" Mark read. "'Animal Transport,' 'Genetic Surgery,' what the hell is genetic surgery?"

"Damned if I know. Maybe gene splicing, though it doesn't sound like that."

"How does 'Local Farmers' fit in with this group?" Anne asked.

"It seems to be reports on observations of the people who live near this special project, wherever it is, mostly just saying that there's no trouble and no interference."

"We don't know where this Leon is working?" Mark asked. "He's not at the headquarters building?"

"Communications from him come in on an outside line," Shirley said, coming over to join them. "It's a dedicated line, with no regular telephone ringer, so we haven't been able to trace it."

"'Disposal,'" Anne said, reading the last of the menu entries. "What's that?"

"Let's look," Paul said, moving the cursor down to that line. He touched a button and yet a new list appeared. He scrolled through it to the bottom. There were only forty entries. He took the last one and displayed it on the screen.

"Remember," he said, "this is a transcription of a voice tape, so some of the words may be wrong." They read the brief entry.

SPEAKER A: We've got another abortion.

SPEAKER B: That's the third one this morning. Can they be used?

SPEAKER A: Total waste. Besides, after a biopsy who wants 'em?

SPEAKER B: All right, tell Leon I'll have someone come down in about an hour.

SPEAKER A: It's the implant forceps [?] I think. The [garbled] can recognize them on sight now.

SPEAKER B: Okay, I'll look into it. How are you disposing of them?

SPEAKER A: Incineration. That's all.

[SPEAKER A: unidentified female, tentatively a technician or lab assistant.]

[SPEAKER B: unidentified male, apparently a liaison between Chang and Leon.]

"And that's all there is?" Mark asked.

"For this one. The same report is in several other files, of course."

"It sure is different from everything else we've been able to pick up from them," Anne said. "This Speaker A called the headquarters just to report an abortion?"

"It's the implant forceps, whatever they are, that they called about, I think. I wish I knew what was going on."

"I wish I knew where they were," Mark said. "About how many pages of printout are there in this set of files?"

"A couple hundred. Not very much."

"I think we need to call in some outside help," Mark went on. He turned to Anne. "Is there anybody at Diger-Fairwell Zoologicals we can trust?" he asked her.

"Yes," she said. "That's a good idea. Paul, how soon can you have a printout?"

"About ten minutes."

"Bring it up to my office, will you?"

"Sure thing."

"Come on, Mark," Anne said, and they left the secret lab.

Anne's office, along with those of the other project directors, was on the second floor. They greeted fellow employees as they got off the elevator, and walked down to her door. If anybody wondered at the strange hours she and the others in the espionage project were keeping these days, nobody asked. Even the company president knew only that they were on a project and not just goofing off.

Anne stopped to speak with her secretary in the outer office. "What are we doing with biofeedback these days?" she asked.

"Nothing, Miss Marino, as far as I know."

"Anything with animals at all?"

"They're doing something with extremely low frequency detection over in Handicapped."

"Excellent. That will do just fine." She and Mark went into the inner office.

"What's that all about?" Mark asked. Technically, Anne was his superior, but for the duration of their espionage, that hardly mattered.

"Just making sure we have some kind of cover story," Anne said, sitting behind her desk and picking up the phone. "Gotta do something about this paperwork," she muttered as she dialed an outside line. She nodded and tapped her ear at the same time, telling Mark that she had detected a tap on the wire.

"Hello, this is Marino over at Data Tronix," she said when her call was answered. "May I speak with Dr. Van Oort, please?"

She waited for the connection to be made, and Mark took a seat.

"Hello, Dr. Van Oort? This is Dr. Marino. Yes. Look, we're having a problem with our E.L.F. studies over here. We're just not used to dealing with animals, and I'd like to come over and talk with you about it for a minute. No, it's rather important. I think we may be damaging some of the animals. Yes, right now will be fine. See you then." She hung up.

"Nobody listening in could make any sense out of that," Mark said dryly.

"I don't think Dr. Van Oort understood any of it either," Anne admitted as Paul walked in carrying a sheaf of printout paper. "But she'll see us. Thanks, Paul, we'll be over at Diger-Fairwell for about an hour or so."

"Okay," Paul said, "you know where to find me." He left and Anne stuffed the printout into a briefcase.

Anne and Mark took a company car out of the parking lot and drove out onto Alexander, then down Cornwallis, but before they got to the big, futuristic Diger-Fairwell building they were stopped by a Visitor checkpoint. Anne, who was driving, handed the guard Mark's ID along with her own and repeated the story about needing to consult on animal encephalography. The guard did not see the briefcase behind the seat and did not insist on searching the car. He handed back their IDs and waved them on.

Dr. Lucia Van Oort turned out to be a very short woman in her midfifties, with short iron-gray hair. She greeted Mark and Anne in her office, but before they could say anything, she suggested they move to another room and led them into what looked like a parlor, with direct access to her office.

"This room, at least," she explained, "is bug free. Please sit down. Dr. Marino, I have no idea what you were talking about on the phone, but I assume it's something you don't want the Visitors to know about."

"That's correct," Anne said. She opened her briefcase and took out the folded stack of printouts. "I can't tell you how we got this," she went on, handing the papers to Dr. Van Oort, "only that it's all transcribed from conversations we've tapped ourselves."

Dr. Van Oort flipped through the pages. "All these speakers are Visitors?" she asked.

"That's right," Mark said. "As you can see, it has something to do with animals, but we just don't know what. Everything else they're doing at their headquarters here has to do with electronics."

"And you obviously want to know what they're up to," Dr. Van Oort said, putting the papers down on a table beside her chair. "It's a matter of familiarity, of course." There was a small intercom on the table. She pressed a button. "Send Carmichal and Hirakawa here, please," she said. "I trust," she went on after releasing the button, "that you'll see fit to take me into your confidence eventually."

"What we don't want to do," Anne explained, "is tell you things that you don't need to know, that might get us or you into trouble if the Visitors ever overhear those things mentioned."

"I understand. I have no desire to learn just how you managed to tap what appears to be in-house communications. But I take it you aren't here just to satisfy your curiosity."

"Of course not. If we can figure out what those papers mean, and how they tie in with the rest of Visitor activity, we'll probably need even more help from you, and you may find yourself more involved than you'd like to be."

"That's as may be," Dr. Van Oort said as a knock sounded at the door. It opened immediately to admit two women.

"Penny Carmichal," Dr. Van Oort said after introductions, "is a herpetologist and geneticist. JoAnn Hirakawa is our top ecologist and a carnivore specialist. More importantly, both can be trusted implicitly." She handed part of the bundle of printouts to Penny, and the rest to JoAnn.

Mark, Anne, and Dr. Van Oort sat silently while the two scientists skimmed through the documents. Penny looked up once at Anne and Mark. "Looks like two kinds of animals," she said. "Seems to be a breeding experiment." Then she went back to her reading.

JoAnn finished first and while waiting for Penny to finish, got up to look out the window. "My first impression," she said without turning around, "is that these animals are native to the Visitors' home planet, not something from Earth."

"Exactly," Penny agreed, still reading.

"Two species," JoAnn went on musingly, "one large, one small. I'd also guess, from what I've read so far, that one is a carnivore"—she turned to face the others—"and the other is a herbivore, the smaller of the two."

"Seems to make sense," Penny said, putting down her bundle and reaching for the one JoAnn had finished. JoAnn, in turn, came back to her seat to read the rest of the reports.

"I didn't know the Visitors had brought any animals with them," Anne said.

"We have reason to believe they did," Dr. Van Oort said, "aside from what you've shown us here. I've not seen any such creatures, but they had to at least have had food stock. Since they eat only live or freshly killed meat, they had to have some animals on board their ships, animals that would eat vegetable matter, be highly efficient in converting that to flesh, and would breed quickly. Something like rabbits or rats, I'd guess."

"A lot of this is totally irrelevant," JoAnn said, flipping through the pages.

"If you say so," Anne said. "We just brought over everything we had."

"Can you get us copies of the tapes?" Penny asked, looking up. "Some of these words you've got marked down as garbled might mean something to us."

"We'll try," Mark said, "but we were stopped on our way over here, and it was just luck that they didn't search the car. Above all, the Visitors must not know that their headquarters has been bugged."

"Good God!" JoAnn said, putting down her papers. "I thought this was just phone conversations you'd listened in on."

"They are," Mark said, "but that represents only about three percent of what we've been picking up lately."

"Does the underground know about this?" Dr. Van Oort asked.

"Not yet," Anne said. "We're doing this on our own. Besides, I don't think they have the people to spare to help out. We're going to have to be our own underground here, I'm afraid."

"We'll have to set up some kind of data drop," Dr. Van Oort said. "I agree it's too risky to just go around carrying the stuff. Where were you stopped?"

"On Cornwallis," Anne said, "between here and Alexander. It was a mobile checkpoint."

"How about cutting through the grounds in back?" Penny suggested. "Behind us is ITA, and Data Tronix is just beyond them, isn't it?"

"As long as we're not observed," Mark said, "that would do, but there's quite a bit of unforested area there."

"I have an aerial survey map from three years ago," Dr. Van Oort said. "We can work out a route and a drop station that won't implicate either of us, or ITA."

"Then let's do it that way," Anne said. "We'll just leave these papers with you. We'd better be getting back now."

"I'll give you a call," Dr. Van Oort said, getting up to show them out. They stopped their conversation as they left the parlor.

"I think your animals will do okay," Dr. Van Oort said as

they crossed her office, "if you just mediate the laryngial tap and use a lower frequency alpha generator."

"Thanks a lot," Mark said. "We'll let you know how things work out."

"Almost time for lunch," Anne said as they rode the elevator down to the main floor, making small talk for the sake of any eavesdroppers.

"Hope they have something good at the cafeteria," Mark said, playing along. They left the building and got into the car.

"Did you really think the elevator might have been bugged?" he asked as Anne drove out onto Cornwallis.

"No sense taking chances. There's our friendly checkpoint again."

The guard pulled them over, and this time he didn't forget to look in the back seat. He had Anne open the briefcase, which contained only a few budgeting papers, then went through the trunk and even looked under the hood. At last he let them go.

"I think we just barely lucked out that time," Mark said as they returned to Data Tronix.

Durk Attweiler medicated only five of his sick goats. The sixth one was doing so poorly that he didn't think it would survive anyway. Might as well save the medication for one it would help.

He went back to the house to fix himself some lunch, and as he ate he couldn't help thinking about what Professor Barnes had said that morning, and about the deer he'd seen going down in the sand. What made it seem more than just a coincidence was the knowledge that the lizards had moved in next door, probably before the incident of the deer, though he hadn't been aware of them at the time. Nor had he been able to observe the Visitors since driving by with his tractor, but the fact that they had chosen to come out here to the country instead of staying near the technology of the Park and Durham seemed to hint that they might be doing something with animals.

Animals that lived in sand, and that dragged people down into it. Maybe deer too. He didn't like the thought of any animal like that living up in the sandy areas just east of his north acres.

After lunch he went back to his goat yard. The sick doe might last another week. Wouldn't even be worth eating, he thought. Perhaps he should put it out of its misery.

He patted the goat on its head, and it bleated weakly. Maybe it would be good for something after all, he thought. He went and got his truck, and put the goat in back. It tried to climb out, so he tied a rope to its horns and tied the ends to either side of the truck. He kept himself from thinking about what he was going to do, but just got in behind the wheel and drove up to his north acres.

He parked near the east fence and got out to look across it to the sandy area beyond. The few trees were tiny and scraggly; there was little brush, almost no grass. The soil was pale, leached, and dry. Soft too, he remembered, almost like beach sand. Moles couldn't live there; their burrows would have collapsed behind them. The sand was deep farther out, and with a very low clay content.

He went back to the truck, untied the goat, and carried it over to the fence. He dropped it over, then climbed after it. The goat wanted to go back into his field, but he didn't let it. Instead, he picked it up and started carrying it toward where the ground got sandier.

A sound overhead made him move back to the dubious shelter of a withered loblolly pine. Coming down from the Research Triangle Park was an alien skyfighter. From its course, it seemed to be heading toward Fayetteville. It passed right overhead, and then slowed, swinging back in an arc.

His truck stood in plain sight, out in the field. The skyfighter passed over it once, then turned to come back again. Quickly, Durk tied the goat to the tree, then walked boldly back toward the fence, hitching up his pants as if he'd just stepped over to relieve himself. He looked up at the skyfighter, hovering twenty feet up, refastened his belt buckle, wiped his hands on his jeans, and reached into the back of the truck for a shovel. The skyfighter turned and sailed off.

Continuing his sham, Durk took the shovel to the fence line and began digging at one of the leaning posts. He straightened the post, packed the dirt back in, then dropped the shovel and went over the fence again.

The goat, in spite of its weakness, was strangely nervous. Durk untied it and carried it onto the sand. When he put the animal down, it tried to go back toward the fence. Durk pulled off his belt and whipped the animal, driving it deeper into the sand barrens. He followed it only a short way.

The goat, weak after this little exertion, and obviously frightened, bent its head to chew at some snake grass. It was facing Durk and did not see the moving mound of sand coming up behind it. As big as a basketball, the mound cruised through the sand, avoiding the trees and plant roots. Durk watched in paralyzed fascination. He hadn't expected anything to happen so soon.

The moving sand mound, now only a hundred feet from the goat, must have made some sound because the animal suddenly raised its head and turned. It bleated once and tried to back away, but the mound accelerated, and suddenly two long snaky tentacles came up from the sand and wrapped themselves around the helpless goat. The goat screamed, and then the tentacles dragged it down under the surface. The sand roiled for a moment, and then was still.

Whatever was under the sand was either eating the goat right there or it was going back deeper, because there was no movement now, no mound skimming just under the surface.

Durk felt something warm and wet running down his pants leg and looked down at himself. He didn't have to just fake taking a leak now, he thought.

He backed away from the spot until he felt his feet on firmer soil. Looking around, he found the tree where he'd left the rope and went to retrieve it. It was hard to do because he couldn't take his eyes off the place where the goat had disappeared. But at last he got his hand on one end and, continuing to back to the fence, coiled the rope sloppily over his arm. He made it over the fence in one step and then ran toward the truck. He didn't remember opening or closing the door. He was just suddenly driving like hell back across his fields. Good, solid clay fields, where no sand-demon could go.

Chapter 4

The skyfighter from the Research Triangle Park landed on the roof of a building next to an enclosed compound. Peter Frye and his four friends were unloaded and marched down a flight of stairs into the building where, although they had been searched and relieved of all personal possessions back at campus, they were searched again. The Visitors did not concern themselves with gender propriety.

When the humiliation was ended, the five students were ushered through the building into a large area like a military compound. The ground was hard and bare, barrackslike buildings stood in rows, and the whole compound was surrounded by a high, heavy-duty chain-link fence with three strands of barbed wire at the top.

Edna was crying, and Dave was trying not to, and Peter didn't feel too cheerful himself. Benny kept a blank face, and Greta was quietly angry.

There were other men and women in the camp, most of them older than Peter and his friends. They stood or walked aimlessly across the bare earth. Beyond the fence to one side were other buildings; these were larger and were contained within their own fences. The other three sides were wilderness, pine scrub, and barren field.

"Welcome to Camp T-3," a tall black man said, coming up to them as they stood there in fear and confusion. His sardonic expression belied the friendliness of his words.

"Where are we?" Peter asked. Edna tried to pull herself

together as two or three other prisoners came up to join them.

"I don't know for sure," the black man said. "Somewhere on the coastal plains—you can tell by the sand." He turned to look around the three sides of the compound that faced the wilderness. "They like their camps to have sand," he said, turning back. "I'm Cliff Upton."

Peter introduced himself and his friends. The three other prisoners, wearing civilian clothes which looked as if they had been doing service for months without a change, nodded in response.

"You the ones that trashed the Visitor liaison office at UNC?" the woman named Susan Green asked.

"Uh, yeah," Dave said. "How'd you hear about it?"

"The lizards don't care who's listening when they talk," Susan answered.

"I need a bathroom," Edna said.

"First door on the left, any building, either end," a man named Bryan Ricardo told her. "Knock before you go in if you're sensitive about that kind of thing."

"Let's get you some bunks," the third man, Chuck Lamont, said. He was quite a bit older than the others, and seemed more resigned to his fate and hence more gentle about it. "You all will want to stick together; there's plenty of room. Come along."

The five students followed him across the compound, with the other three prisoners walking beside them.

"What's going to happen?" Greta asked. Her eyes kept searching the fence, checking out the scrub and brush beyond the chain link.

"Today," Cliff said, "nothing. Tomorrow you'll be tested and maybe put to work in one of those buildings over there." He jerked his head at the larger buildings behind them.

"Food's not bad," Chuck said, "if you're a vegetarian. No meat for the prisoners. You'll get plenty to eat, however."

"How long have you been here?" Dave asked him.

"Since the camp opened about three months ago." They came to one of the barracks buildings. "But I was arrested two weeks after the Visitors first came to Earth. I've seen a lot of people come and go."

"When will they set our sentences?" Peter asked as they entered the barracks. Bunks lined both walls. There were no lockers. They paused a moment while Edna stepped into the small bathroom, which smelled.

"You gotta be kidding," Susan Green said. "You stay here as long as they want you. You leave only when they find some use for you."

"You have to realize," Bryan said, "you have no rights here at all. As far as the lizards are concerned, we're just animals. They keep us this well because it serves their purposes, not because of any human feeling."

"Anybody ever escape?" Greta asked.

"Nope," Cliff said.

"That fence looks easy to climb," Greta went on.

"It is," Chuck said, glancing at his companions. Edna came out and they went to find their bunks.

"Then how come you don't try to get out?" Greta wanted to know.

"Did you see that strip of bare sand around the compound, just outside the fence?"

"They keep dogs out there?"

"Something like that. Some fool gives us a demonstration every couple of days. You wait until you see before you try making a break. Here you go, five bunks together. Supper will be in about an hour and a half. Why don't you just set here a spell and get used to the idea that you're not going anywhere the lizards don't want you to go? We'll be outside."

The four prisoners nodded at the young newcomers and went on out the door at the other end of the barracks. Edna, unable to control herself further, threw herself down on a bunk, sobbing.

* * *

Dr. Lucia Van Oort poured the last of the Hennesy into two snifters, put them on a tray, and carried them into the bedroom where her husband, Ralph, was already under the sheet. "It's going to be Sebastiani after this," she said, handing him one of the glasses.

Ralph put down the papers he was shuffling through so that he could swirl the brandy in his glass. "Maybe we ought to switch to bourbon," he said.

Lucia took a sip of her own brandy and was just about to get into bed when the doorbell rang. She exchanged glances with her husband. It was nearly ten o'clock, and these days few people went calling at that hour.

"I'll get it," Ralph said. He threw off the sheet, threw on a robe, and walked down the hall to the living room. After only a moment's hesitation, Lucia put her own robe back on and followed him.

Ralph opened the front door and over his still-broad shoulders Lucia could see Penny Carmichal and JoAnn Hirakawa on the front step. Ralph let them in quickly, then closed and relocked the door.

"Sorry we got you out of bed," JoAnn said as they all moved into the living room. "We didn't want to call; I think the phone line's tapped again."

"That's all right," Lucia said. "Would you like some coffee?"

"No thanks," Penny said. "We're not going to stay any longer than we have to. Ever since those students broke into the UNC liaison offices, the lizards have been tighter with their security than usual. We got stopped twice on our way over here."

"Were you searched?" Ralph asked with some concern. He didn't know the purpose of their visit, but it was obvious to him that they wouldn't be here except on important business that the Visitors might like to learn about.

"Both times," JoAnn said, "but we brought nothing with us. Except this." She held out an envelope that had been torn open. Lucia took it and looked inside. It contained an official-looking but totally specious memo to the effect that

Lucia's withholding figures had been found to be in error and the payroll department wanted to set things straight first thing in the morning. "You, uh, forgot to take this with you when you left," JoAnn added, to fill Lucia in on their cover in case she was asked.

"Thanks," Lucia said dryly. "I'll see to it, of course. So, could you make any sense out of that report?"

"I think I'll go back to bed," Ralph said. "The less I know about this the better." With a nod at the two younger scientists, he left the room.

"There's really not much to say," JoAnn said when she heard the bedroom door close. "But the implications are disturbing."

"We sorted through everything twice," Penny went on, "including a few new messages somebody left at the drop behind ITA. The Visitors are engaged in a breeding program for sure, involving two separate species of animals. All indications are that both species are alien."

"As we had first guessed," JoAnn continued, "the smaller species is a herbivore. The factors they're looking for are a high rate of breeding, efficient conversion of plant matter to animal protein, and adaptability to a range of environments we haven't figured out yet."

"I'd guess," Lucia said, "that that's their basic food stock. Any idea what it's like?"

"Mammalian," Penny said. "Size somewhere between a house cat and a cocker spaniel. Litters four times a year, six to ten pups each time. Diurnal, easily managed, no by-products noted."

"Seems like a perfectly reasonable project," Lucia said. "Lord knows we can't keep them fed with our own animals. What about the other species?"

"Carniverous," JoAnn said. "Maybe the size of a burro or donkey. We think it's reptilian, but we can't be sure. We know at least that it's hairless. And this is the disturbing part. The lizards seem to be trying for size, strength, speed, and ferocity. What the hell do the Visitors need attack animals for?"

"I'm sure I have no idea, but maybe Dr. Marino can fit that in with whatever else she's been learning about their activities. Is that all?"

"For right now," Penny said. "We'd thought you'd better know, in case Marino and Casey told you more that helps make sense out of all this."

"You know just as much as I do," Lucia said, "but thanks for coming by." She got up and led them to the front door. "Be careful going home."

When they were gone she went back to the bedroom, slipped out of her robe, and got under the sheet. She sipped idly at her brandy while Ralph, having put aside his papers again, watched her quietly.

"Wolves," Lucia said, half to herself. "Why would they want to breed wolves?"

It was shortly after eight o'clock in the morning when Durk Attweiler came to the intersection of Columbia and Cameron, where three days ago he'd seen the unfortunate students being loaded into an alien paddywagon. This time, instead of driving by, he turned right on Cameron and entered the campus. Though classes had already started, there were still a number of students walking along the street. Durk pulled over to the curb, rolled down the window on the passenger side, and called out to a young fellow who looked like a football player.

"Excuse me," he said. "I'm trying to find, uh, Professor Morton Barnes."

"Don't know him," the student called back. "Go up to the second driveway on the right, and you'll be right next to Memorial. Information is inside."

"Thanks," Durk called. He went as directed, parked in a visitor's parking space ("Small v on that," he muttered to himself), and went up the stairs to the building's front door. He felt conspicuous in his old, worn clothes. There was a time, he knew, when jeans and such were popular attire among college students, but now few people wore other than slacks and sport shirts. One of the girls who'd been arrested yesterday, he remembered, had affected a pseudo-farm style. He put the thought out of his mind.

Inside, to the left of the door, was an office with a sign above the door identifying it as the place he wanted. A woman behind a desk looked up as he entered and smiled, though the smile was strained. At first Durk thought she was disapproving of him, but then he remembered again the troubles of three days ago.

"I'm looking for Professor Morton Barnes—I think," Durk said, unsure of himself.

"Just a moment," the woman said, and opened a campus directory. "His office is room three-oh-nine, the Smythe Building. Do you know where that is?"

"No, I surely don't."

"Here." She took out a map printed on a single sheet of paper and turned it toward him on the desk. "You're here," she said, marking a building with a red x. "Smythe is just across the way here." She marked another building.

"Okay. Uh, can I leave my truck here?"

"Surely, and you can keep the map."

"Thank you." He nodded and left.

He could see Smythe from the steps, across Cameron and set back sixty yards from it. Folding the map and putting it in his pocket, he started across the street, watching for traffic, of which there was little, and Visitors, of which there were none that he could see. The first door he tried in Smythe led into a classroom where a lecture was in progress. Embarrassed, he backed out and went around the side to another door, this one giving access to a lobby with stairs running up both sides.

Room 309 was at the north end of the third floor. The professor's name was on the door, and it was open a crack. Durk paused, caught his breath, settled his determination, and knocked at the door frame.

"Come on in," he heard the professor answer. No secretary? Durk slid inside, more self-conscious than ever about his clothes and the faint aroma of barnyard that clung to him.

"Professor Barnes?" he said. "I'm Durk Attweiler. We sort of met a couple days ago at the FCX."

"Ah, yes, I remember. You witnessed those unfortunate students being taken off."

"Yes, sir. You said something about some kind of animal they have guarding those prison camps those kids will be sent to."

"Ye-e-s, at least that's what Kenny Borgman told me in his letter."

"Well, I think there may be one of those things in the sand fields near my farm."

"Indeed. And what makes you think so?"

"Couple weeks ago I saw a deer out there, and it just disappeared, sucked right down into the ground. Kinda frightening, but what the hell, maybe I wasn't seeing things right. It was a ways off. But then three days ago, after hearing what you said, I took a goat up to the same place. Just a sick one, it woulda died in a couple of weeks anyway. Took it across the fence and drove it out onto the sand flats."

"Just a minute," Barnes said. He got up from his desk, went around to the door, looked out into the hall, and then closed it carefully. "Sit down," he said, all trace of condescension gone. "What happened to the goat?"

Durk sat on the edge of a chair. "You see those movies about submarines? How they come along under the water, and all you see is a wake moving toward the enemy ship? Well, it was just like that, only it was coming through the sand."

"What was?"

"I don't know. But it came awfully quickly. And when it got to the goat, two big snaky arms came up out of the sand and grabbed the goat and dragged it down."

"How far were you from the goat?"

"Maybe thirty feet. With the deer, there were bushes in the way, and I couldn't see the ground so clear. But this time I wanted to make sure. I don't know what that thing was, but it sure as hell knew the goat was there, and took it. I didn't see it going back."

"How long were the tentacles?" Barnes asked, scribbling on a sheet of paper.

"I couldn't say for sure—six or seven feet or so. They didn't have suckers on 'em as far as I could see. Is that the same kind of critter they've got guarding the prison camps?"

"It sounds like it, Mr. Attweiler. Why did you decide to tell *me* about it?"

"You were talking about it and I overheard your name. I didn't know who else to go to."

"I see. Very well, Mr. Attweiler, I *do* know people to go to, and I'll tell them about this." He wrote a few more words and then stood up. "Thank you for coming to see me," he said, extending his hand.

"Sure thing, Professor," Durk answered, getting to his feet as well. "I just felt somebody ought to know." He accepted the proffered hand, then turned and left the office.

Morton Barnes watched him leave, then sat back down in his chair. The farmer had been right. If one of those prison animals had escaped, somebody ought to do something about it. He picked up his phone.

"I'm going out for a while," he told the office secretary when she answered. "Cancel any appointments until after lunch." He hung up and fingered the notes he'd made. He started to put the paper in his pocket, then decided against it. Better not have anything like that on him if he got stopped at a checkpoint. He went down to the parking lot, got in his car, and headed toward highway 54 and the Research Triangle Park. The people at Diger-Fairwell Zoologicals, he thought, would have a better idea of what to do with this information than anybody else in the area.

Leon and two of his assistants, Vivian and Edmond, drove the special car with balloon tires along the newly made track through the second-growth forest between their laboratory complex and the sand barrens to the north. While

Edmond drove, Leon examined the map folder, comparing its symbols with the actual terrain.

"You can see right here," Vivian said, riding on the flat bed behind, "where the soil changes character. Still lots of clay, but it's being replaced by quartz rock and red gravel. The trees are all shorter and spindlier. At the bottom of the slope"—she pointed in their direction of travel—"the sand takes over completely." Behind her were bolted several large instruments for taking readings on the depth and quality of the soil over which they traveled.

"Looks almost like some places I've seen back home," Edmond said as they neared the sand fields. "Except for the plants, of course."

"Let's follow the perimeter to the right," Leon suggested as they drove onto the sandy area. "I want a detailed analysis of the entire margin."

Edmond drove more slowly as Vivian turned to the control panels and readouts on the bulky instruments. She switched them on, and they emitted a soft hum. "A little more to the right," she told Edmond, who steered the vehicle so that they rode right above the edge of the sand.

"Let me have the earphones," he said, coming to a stop. Vivian handed him a pair, and he set them on his head. With these, he could hear the probe echoes as they came up from the ground, and according to the volume and pitch, he could steer the vehicle precisely, instead of having to depend on visual clues, which could be misleading.

Vivian gave Leon another wire with a jack at the end, which he plugged into the map folder. As Edmond drove them slowly along the margin of the sand fields, depth and density data under the vehicle and for several yards on either side were translated into a graphic image which was superimposed over the map and stored within the folder's memory.

The sand-lake margin was surprisingly regular for about a third of the way around its circumference. As they approached the north, where the fine porous gravel replaced the clay, the border became less distinct and they had to go more slowly. Leon wanted to make sure that there was no way out of the sand fields, or that if there was it could be cut off without too much difficulty. He had six of his experimental animals in there now, and while they were too large to get through any gaps the initial survey might have missed, the females would be birthing soon, and the young ones could easily escape.

They found no gaps, but on the west side the sand and clay mixed in a way that was less than optimum. Though denser than the animals liked, it would be possible for a strong male or a large female to force its way through, especially if it were hungry enough, and if the soil dried out any further. As they now rode south just inside the fence line between them and their farmer neighbor to the west, Leon made special note of the quality and depth of the soil.

"We may need to put in a barricade along here," he said to Vivian.

"I've got that already under consideration," the technician told him. "I don't think we need to hurry, though. The friable soil is only about four feet deep, and far too dense for pups. It does extend quite a way into that field there, but if we keep the animals well fed, they shouldn't come up here at all."

"We'll want this section well secured by next spring, however," Leon said. "Fall and winter rains will keep them where the drainage is better, but when we have thirty or forty half-grown youngsters, they'll feel cramped and will try anywhere."

"I figure four hundred yards of comb rod will do it," Vivian said as Edmond followed the signals away from the fence line and back toward a portion of the perimeter with a more distinct interface.

They finished the rest of the circuit quickly and headed back to the house. Leon left his two technicians to put the vehicle away, and went upstairs to his office, where Freda was waiting for him.

"Here's the report on Attweiler," she said, handing him another folder.

"Good. And here's the update on the sand-fields perimeter." He gave her the map and she left to integrate it with her main data file.

Leon sat at his desk, opened the folder, and touched the "on" icon. The left half of the folder showed several pictures of Durk Attweiler, while the right half was filled with alien text. He did no more than read the summary, though the report itself was several thousand words long. In brief, Durk Attweiler was a bachelor, almost forty years old, and his family had lived on that farm for over one hundred fifty years. He'd served in the Army, had one year of college education, and was on the thin edge of poverty. Quiet, solitary, with few friends.

Leon looked at the pictures. Yes, he'd seen the man before, up at that tavern that Chang had taken him to. He put the folder away, relieved that his closest neighbor offered so little to worry about.

Chapter 5

It was getting on toward lunch, but Morton Barnes didn't dare call his secretary to tell her he would be late getting back to campus. And after what he'd learned from Dr. Van Oort and her two assistants during the last half hour, he was sorry he'd come here at all.

The four of them sat in Lucia's private parlor adjacent to her office at Diger-Fairwell. "Crivits," Lucia said. "At least we have a name for them."

"That's what Kenny Borgman called them," Morton said. "Guard animals that burrow through the sand trenches around their prison camps."

"No Earth reptile has tentacles such as you describe," Penny said, "but that doesn't mean that such creatures can't exist. Of course they might not be reptiles; they could be mollusks."

"I think that question is rather academic," Lucia said. "The real question is, why this secret breeding project? I'd think the animals would do just fine where they are normally kept."

"It's monstrous," Morton Barnes said. "Breeding food animals I can understand. But predators! You don't suppose they intend to set them loose on us, do you?"

"That doesn't seem very likely," JoAnn said. "These crivits need a very specialized environment. The Visitors have to dig trenches around their camps and fill them with

75

sand just for that purpose. Crivits would be as helpless in the heavy clay soils around here as a shark would."

"We need more information," Lucia said. She turned to Barnes. "Now that we have something concrete to tell our sources," she said, "they should be able to dig more data out of what they're recording."

"Fine," Morton said, "but I don't want to know about it."

"You don't need to know any more than you do," Lucia told him. "But we need just a little bit more from you. You don't have to name names, but it would help if we knew where this informant of yours saw the crivit."

Barnes stared at her blankly for a moment. "I haven't the slightest idea where he lives," he said at last. "He just walked into my office this morning because he'd overheard me talking about Kenny Borgman at the FCX a few days ago."

"Do you know his name?"

"Yes, I do. All right, do you have phone books for the area?"

"Raleigh, Durham, Chapel Hill, right there on the sideboard," Lucia said. Morton went over to them and flipped through.

"He's not listed anywhere," he said. "Look, I'm going to have to get back to campus. I'm already going to be late for a one o'clock lecture, and I haven't had lunch yet. I'll see what I can find out and let you know."

"We'd appreciate it," Lucia said. "But be careful when you call."

"I will. I'll figure something out." Hurriedly he got to his feet and departed.

"I'll write up a report," Penny said, "and take it over to the drop this evening."

"I didn't want to frighten Professor Barnes," Lucia said, going over to the phone, "but I don't think we can wait for that." She dialed a number. "May I speak to Dr. Marino, please," she asked when the call was answered. She waited a moment, then, "Anne, Lucia here. How about lunch today? That'd be fine, see you there."

"Try to get hold of any information you can on crivits," she told her assistants as they left the parlor. "Needless to say, take no chances."

"You be careful too," Penny cautioned.

The one advantage to a fast-food place, Anne Marino thought as she and Mark Casey walked into the McDonald's, was that even if it were bugged, there was so much conversation and noise going on, nobody could make much sense out of what they heard.

Lucia Van Oort was already seated when they took their orders into the main room. "I know at least part of what Leon's up to," Lucia said as they took their seats, then told them what she and her assistants had learned from Professor Barnes.

"I'm afraid I can't appreciate all the implications," Mark said around a mouthful of hamburger, "but knowing that much will help us assign some meaning to some of the other transcriptions we've got."

"One thing's for sure," Anne said. "They wouldn't be doing that kind of research here if they didn't want it secret, and if it weren't important. When we know where their breeding station is, I think we should go down and check it out."

"Do you dare take that chance?" Lucia asked.

"The more we know about what's going on," Mark said, "the better we'll be able to do something to counter not only this project, but anything else the Visitors are doing. You know from your own experience just how constrained we are in everything we do. Part of the reason for this whole espionage bit is to figure out a way to defeat their surveillance, diminish their control, and reduce their effectiveness. We can't throw the lizards off by force of arms; that's been tried. Even the toxin that the people in L.A. put into the atmosphere was only partially effective. We've got to find some other way."

"I agree, of course," Lucia said. "I don't need to tell you that we have a project or two of our own that we're working on. I'm sure every company in the Research Triangle has some kind of angle. But if you go down snooping around, you may jeopardize not only your own safety, but that of everybody else if you get caught."

"But if we don't go," Anne said, "then we learn nothing. You've seen what kind of information we can get from phone taps. Thin. Useful, but thin. What really helps is comparing that with firsthand observation. Like comparing a satellite radar image of the ground with a field survey. Without the survey, you don't know what the radar images mean. It's got to be done."

"If you just happen to pick up one of these crivits," Lucia said, "or one of the other animals they have down there, do bring it back, will you?"

"We'll sure give it a try," Mark said.

Morton Barnes did not get his lunch and did not make his lecture. Instead, as soon as he got back to campus shortly after one o'clock, he went straight to the Geology Department and went in to see Mary Kennedy, an old friend who specialized in North Carolina land formations.

"Don't ask me why," he said after a hurried greeting, "but I need to know about particularly sandy areas around here, within, say, twenty miles or so of Chapel Hill."

"Shouldn't be too hard to find out," Mary said, getting up to go to a large map case and pulling out a drawer. "You look frightened, Morton."

"I am. Look, you don't want to know."

"Nothing to do with our Visitors, I hope," Mary said, taking several large-scale maps out and laying them down on top of the counter.

"Mary, if I told you anything, you'd wish I hadn't." He came over to look over her shoulder. The maps were barely recognizable as being of Orange, Durham, Alamance, Chatham, and Churchill counties. Instead of the familiar highways and cities, each map was composed of irregular shapes of different colors and combinations of colors.

He felt her eyes on him and looked up from the multicolored surface.

"Those students," she started to say.

"Mary, be still. I'm sorry, I mean it. Look, maybe there's no danger, I don't know. But if there is, I want to get this over with as quickly as possible. Now show me, where is there a lot of sand?"

She continued to stare at him. "If you want sand," she said slowly, "you go to the beaches. And then there's the sand-hills region around Fort Bragg and Fayetteville."

"Too far. Within twenty miles, or ten more likely. Close enough for somebody to drive from there to Chapel Hill at seven in the morning without putting himself out."

At last she returned her gaze to the maps. "All right," she sighed. She scanned the first one, then flipped it aside to look at the one beneath. "Right here," she said, pointing. "Northeast corner of Churchill County, several hundred acres of alluvial sand, Carolina gravel, trapped in an ancient rocky quartz formation. Will that do?"

"Any farming possible in that area?" Morton asked. He took out an old envelope and started noting down names, highway numbers, and other landmarks.

"All of it's pretty poor," Mary said. "Look, Morton, if you have sand, you can't have a good farm."

"Doesn't have to be good. Thanks a lot, Mary. I'll tell you about it later, if I can."

Back in his office, Morton Barnes stared for a long time at the scribbled notes on the back of the envelope. Maybe, he thought, he was just being paranoid. But if Dr. Van Oort had been so careful about eavesdropping and bugs, who was he to just assume that his office, or Mary Kennedy's office, was free of surveillance? If the Visitors were spying on him, he just hoped they hadn't overheard his conversation with the geologist, or if they had that they wouldn't understand what had been said and implied.

He looked at his phone. He would have to make the call, either that or drive down to Churchill County in person.

Of course, he thought with a sinking stomach, if his office was bugged, his talk with Durk Attweiler this morning was more than sufficient to get him into trouble. The fact that the Visitors hadn't approached him about it yet was no reassurance.

At last he picked up the phone, got information, and asked for Durk Attweiler's number. The operator gave it to him, he thanked her and hung up. He dialed the number, and the phone rang and rang. Just as he was about to decide that Attweiler was out in his fields somewhere, the farmer answered.

"Mr. Attweiler, this is Professor Barnes."

"Yes, sir," Attweiler said, "what can I do for you?"

"It's about that livestock," Barnes said. "I think I may have a buyer for you."

"Uh, right," Attweiler answered, and even over the phone Barnes could hear the tension in his voice. "They want to take a look at it?"

"They can't very well make you an offer until they see what you have. No need to bring it up here, though. We can come down and meet you some time this afternoon if that would be all right."

"You don't know how to get to my place. I'll be at the Five Star Bar at three."

"That would be perfect. I won't be coming down myself, but they'll know how to find you." He said a few words more and rang off.

Well, he thought, he was committed now. He felt like some kind of secret agent, talking in code like that. Probably a waste of time, might as well just come out and say what he meant.

He flipped through the Research Triangle Park section of the Chapel Hill phone book until he found Dr. Van Oort's number. But caution got the better of him. Maybe his own safety was compromised, but there was no sense in letting anybody else know that Dr. Van Oort had anything to do with this business. He went back downstairs and up to Franklin Street. There were phone booths in the arcade between the North Carolina National Bank offices and Papagayo's restaurant. He called from there.

"I've found your livestock," he said without introducing himself, and gave instructions on how to meet Attweiler. Dr. Van Oort just said "thank you" when he'd finished, and hung up.

And that takes care of that, Barnes thought as he walked back to campus. Either he was damned, or he was off the hook, but he wouldn't have to get involved in this business any further.

Lucia Van Oort did her own spell of thinking before calling Anne Marino at Data Tronix. She wanted to convey the message clearly without giving anything away to the eavesdropper she knew would be listening in. At last she dialed the number and asked for Dr. Marino.

"Anne," she said, "Lucia here. I feel like breaking off early. Would you and Mark like to meet me at the Five Star Bar at three for a couple drinks?"

"I'm sorry," Anne said. "There's no way we can get away right now. We've got visitors." She didn't have to capitalize the last word for Lucia to get the message.

"Another time, then," Lucia said, and hung up in a cold sweat. Visitors in the offices? she wondered, or just watching the building from outside? She dialed an inside line. "Penny, could you come up here please?"

Peter Frye hadn't seen much of his friends that day. Right after breakfast the five students, along with maybe twenty other new prisoners, had been marched to a building in the adjacent compound where they'd been given a battery of intelligence and personality tests while hooked up to some kind of EEG machine. As the testing progressed, one after another was told that they were through, and led away, while those remaining went on to further questions. When they were through with the two-hour-long session, only four other prisoners besides Benny, Greta, Dave, and Edna were left. He didn't know if that was good or bad.

But he didn't have time to talk it over with the others, because they were immediately separated and taken to other buildings. Peter was put in charge of a machine which created the marvelously elastic fabric from which Visitor uniforms were made. He was convinced, because of the mindlessness of the job, that it was either just make-work, or another form of test. All he had to do was watch a bank of gauges, and whenever a needle went from the blue into the orange, he had to press a button. He hardly ever saw samples of the finished product.

Lunch had proved to be substantial, if totally vegetarian. He saw Edna at another table, and wanted to join her, but the guards forbade it. But after lunch there was some free time, during which he could mingle with the other prisoners in the main compound.

Not that there was anything to do. He got a chance to talk with Cliff Upton and Chuck Lamont for a while, but they could give him little information on how the camp was run. Apparently, the Visitors gave their prisoners a different routine every day. It seemed to make no sense.

He and Greta were watching as a skyfighter landed on the roof of the receiving building, and were wondering what new prisoners might be coming in when speakers around the compound began calling out names. Those called, including Peter but not Greta, were directed through a fenced walkway to yet another building, where they were put into individual cubicles. These were just four-by-four feet, with only a chair in the middle, bolted to the floor and facing what looked like a full-wall window. If it was transparent, he couldn't see what was on the other side, since the glass was dark and no light from the cubicle passed through to illuminate what was beyond.

Colored lights suddenly started playing down on him

from the ceiling, and after a moment he seemed to drift into a kind of confused dream, of which he could remember very little later. When he was released, he was taken back to the main compound. There he saw the new prisoners with Susan Green, Bryan Ricardo, and several others. He went over to join them.

"What the hell did they do to me just now?" he asked the older prisoners, interrupting the conversation in progress. He briefly described his experience in the cubicle.

"You've just had your first session at conversion," Susan told him. "Whether you get another depends on how well they liked your performance this time."

"Is that good or bad?"

"Depends. If you can't be converted, you stay here, they don't make you work a lot, and they feed you very well. If you can, they eventually take you somewhere else."

"I don't know if I like the sound of that," one of the new prisoners said. "I've heard that the lizards eat people."

"Ridiculous," Bryan said.

Durk Attweiler liked Arnold Rutgers immediately. The surgical veterinarian from Diger-Fairwell was a tall, craggy man in his late forties, with hands that were both strong and gentle, and he had a way with animals. JoAnn Hirakawa, on the other hand, was terse, slightly sardonic, and not easy to talk with.

They'd met him at the Five Star right on time and with only the briefest of explanations of who they were, followed his truck to his farm. There Arnold had loosened up a bit, to say only that the people at Diger-Fairwell were very interested in the sand creature he had seen, and just wanted to get a firsthand view of it. He had surprised Durk by opening the back of their station wagon and taking out a small pig.

"Figured you'd have only so many goats to spare," Arnold said.

"If you can show us where you saw the creature," JoAnn said, "we'd like to see if it will take the bait."

"You're not going to like it," Durk told her. "Neither is the pig."

"It's sedated," Arnold said. "It's also a breed we use for a lot of our medical testing, and is very easily controlled. This kind of experiment is not one that would receive government approval, but under the circumstances, I can't think of a better way to find out if what you've got up there in the sand fields is the same as the creatures the Visitors use to guard their prison camps."

"Let's go do it," JoAnn said, going back to the station wagon.

"We'd better use my truck," Durk said. "The lizards fly over sometimes, and if they see that wagon, they'll wonder what the hell is going on. In fact, you'd better park it in the barn. I'll put the pig in the truck."

He took the animal from Arnold, who went to move the station wagon, and fitted a halter around its neck. It was a very small pig, little more than a foot high at the shoulder, and quiet, but he didn't want it jumping out on their way to the sand fields. JoAnn watched silently as he lifted the pig into the back of his truck and fastened the two lead lines to either side.

"I'll ride in back with it," Arnold offered as he came back from the barn. He climbed over the tailgate while JoAnn got into the passenger's seat.

"You're taking this pretty seriously," Durk said to JoAnn as he started the cranky engine.

"Aren't you?"

"I live next to them. I have to."

"We all live next to them these days, one way or another," she said. There was no further conversation until they got to his north acres.

He parked the truck next to the fence, a couple of hundred feet south of where he'd gone over the day before.

As Arnold untied the pig, Durk took out some shovels, fence posts, and a coil of wire which he'd stowed in back.

"Just in case somebody comes by," he explained, "you're going to help me reset this section of fence."

"You're awfully cautious," JoAnn said.

"It's something you learn," he answered, "if you augment your living the way I do."

Arnold handed him the pig. "Mountain crafts?" he asked with feigned innocence.

"Of a sort." He met Arnold's eyes and knew that the man understood perfectly. JoAnn, on the other hand, was at a complete loss.

"Let's go over here," Durk went on. "That way we'll have the cover of the trees, such as it is, if a flyer goes by."

"Do they often?" JoAnn asked.

"Every now and then. Nearly got caught with the goat."

The fence wires at that point were so slack that they had no trouble going through. Arnold carried the pig, insisting it needed no rope or halter. Durk led them diagonally up toward the sand fields, where they paused at the edge of the more barren area.

"It might not be here now," Arnold said. "Or it might not be hungry."

"One way to find out," Durk said.

Arnold put the pig down, faced its snout toward the center of the sand fields, and gave its rump a good, hard smack. The pig squealed, scampered away through the low weedy plants, and halted about a hundred feet from them. Its feet sank nearly up to its hocks in the soft sand.

"Don't watch the pig," Durk said. "Watch the ground beyond it." He pointed off toward the east and south.

They saw it then, like a bubble moving through the sand. It turned to bypass the roots of the few low bushes and plants, but otherwise headed straight toward the pig.

"That's a crivit, all right," Arnold said softly. The pig seemed oblivious to the approaching danger until the last moment. Then the moving disturbance in the sand accelerated, the pig squealed as if it had been stuck, and two tentacles shot up out of the sand, wrapped themselves around the pig's struggling body, and dragged it down.

"That's a crivit all right," Arnold said again, only this time his voice was strained.

"Shit," JoAnn said. "Shit, shit." The sand where the pig had been churned for a moment, and then was still.

"Let's get out of here," Durk said. "This ground's pretty firm, but I don't trust anything that can burrow like that."

They nearly ran to the fence, and Durk and Arnold had to help JoAnn over. She was trembling, and her skin was white and clammy.

"I've seen wolves pull down an elk," she said. "I've seen wildcats rip up rabbits. I've seen foxes and cats eat mice, and hawks eat snakes. But this, I don't think I can stand this."

"If you've seen what you want to see," Durk said, "we'd better get back to the house." He walked back to the truck and had his stuff loaded into the back by the time the others joined him.

"We're going to have to capture one of those monsters," Arnold said.

"How you going to do it?" Durk asked.

"I don't know. We'll figure something out. But right now I could sure use a good stiff drink."

"I may have just the thing for you," Durk said.

Freda drove the ground car into the headquarters parking lot at the Research Triangle Park. The only problem with her position as Leon's second on the project was that the hours were so long. She was ravenously hungry, and appreciated Darin for waiting for her when he could have eaten hours ago.

She entered the large building by the front door, to which she had a key, and found Darin waiting for her in the lobby. They greeted each other with a brief and discreet embrace, and then Darin escorted her to his suite on the second floor.

"If he keeps on working you like this," Darin said as they went through the all but silent halls, "Leon ought to apply for a larger staff."

"Three more people would be ideal," Freda agreed. "But I don't think we're likely to get any help until he starts showing some results."

Darin let her into his suite, which consisted of a single large sitting room, a bedroom, and a bath.

"This is what I really miss," Freda said, throwing herself on a couch. "You've seen those rooms we have at the farm. So small you can hardly move."

"I guess that's not likely to change," Darin said, going to the far end of the room where tastefully decorated cages covered two full shelves next to the stainless steel personal abattoir. "Something to drink before supper?"

"I'm acquiring a taste for beer," Freda said with a wry chuckle. "Leon keeps the farm well stocked. But wine will be just fine."

"No, I have some beer, I think," Darin said. He opened the refrigerator and took out two cans with different labels. "Can you tell the difference?" he asked, holding them up so she could see them.

"Not really. You know, I'm getting a rather funny feeling about this whole project."

"You mean," Darin said, handing her one of the cans, "lack of proper facilities, inadequate staff, and no direct link with any Mother Ship, let alone Diana's?" His tone was lightly sarcastic.

"That's it exactly. On the one hand, we're supposed to be doing something important enough to warrant a separate laboratory; on the other hand it's just not enough of a laboratory to do much."

"That fact has not escaped Chang's notice," Darin said. He took a long pull at his beer, then went back to the cages. "At the same time," he went on, "there's no doubt that Diana has personally approved the project. Verlog tonight?"

"Anything, I'm starved. Yes, verlog will be fine." She drank her beer, slouched down on the couch, and closed her eyes. "You know what I think?" she asked rhetorically. "I think Leon's taking advantage of being allowed to do a small project to do more than he has been authorized. I think he's trying to prove himself to Diana by doing more than he was asked, working beyond the call of duty."

"Makes sense," Darin said. He reached into a cage and took out an animal the size of a very large house cat. It had short fur, and face like a rabbit's, but with small, round ears. Its feet had short but strong black claws like a squirrel's, and its legs seemed as adapted to tree climbing as to ground walking. The animal did not resist, but hung limply in his grasp. He carried it over to the stainless steel counter of the abattoir.

There, holding it by the back of the neck so that its head was over the recessed bowl, he took down a knife like a large scalpel and slit the creature's throat. The animal kicked ineffectively as its blood poured into the bowl. When its movement stilled, Darin removed the head completely and took an elastic tie and wrapped it around the animal's hind legs. Then he hung it up from the hook above the bowl so that it could continue to drain.

"At least I'm covered," Freda said, getting up from the couch. The smell of hot blood was making her stomach growl. "I've documented everything I've done, every order I've received; it's a model of record keeping. If Leon gets into trouble by overreaching himself, I can prove that I was just following orders, and on occasion did so under protest. But if he succeeds, there's nothing in the file to discredit me with Leon either."

"There's nothing more dangerous," Darin said, leaning back against the counter while the verlog dripped, "than an ambitious superior."

"Ambition's not so bad," Freda said, "but when it's coupled with behind-the-back political maneuvering—"

"Well, that's what I meant." Darin took down the verlog

and with the scalpel-like knife quickly skinned it. Then, just to be fancy, he removed all the flesh from the bones and arranged the strips of still-warm meat on a platter. He put the skelton with viscera, the skin, and the head into the disposal unit at the back of the abattoir while Freda got glass mugs from a cabinet into which she poured the still-fresh blood.

They carried their repast over to the table in the middle of the room and sat down. Darin picked up one of the mugs and raised it in toast.

"Here's to Leon," he said. "May he get away with whatever he's up to, to everybody's profit."

"I'll drink to that," Freda said, and took a sip of the blood. "Needs a little salt," she said.

It was a week later, late enough in the evening by now that the staff cafeteria at Diger-Fairwell was nearly empty. Only a few snackers taking a moment off from the night shift sat at the round tables. Arnold Rutgers, with his two guests, Anne Marino and Mark Casey, were the only group and were seated right in the middle of the large room.

"We seem to have an interesting situation down there," Mark said, working his way through his third piece of cherry pie. "We ran a global search on every communication we've recorded so far, both in-house and outside, trying to find references to crivits, breeding, Leon, and so forth. There were a lot fewer than we expected."

"We've confirmed," Anne expanded, "that Leon is here at Diana's request, and that he is in fact supposed to be working with crivits, but the reports he's sent to her so far talk only about metabolic adaptation to Earth's environment."

"Nothing about breeding at all?" Arnold asked. He swirled the rest of the cold coffee in his cup.

"Only in the sense of providing subjects for study, not in the sense of enhancing or developing physical characteristics," Anne said. "Of course, we may have missed some implications, and your own people will be able to interpret those messages better. We didn't dare bring the printouts with us, but they're at the drop right now."

"So how do we know Leon is up to any more than what he says?" Arnold asked.

"Just a few casual communications," Mark said, "between Leon's assistant and someone at headquarters named Darin. Even Chang is not being told the whole story."

"You could be misinterpreting," Arnold said. "Biological jargon can be just as opaque as that used by computer scientists."

"There's nothing opaque," Anne said, "about Freda telling Darin, just in passing as they're arranging to meet this evening, that Leon won't have to cull the weak crivits from his stock, since the strong ones are doing it for him, and that they'll need to bring in some more to keep their numbers up."

"I don't want to argue with you," Arnold said, "but I'll reserve judgment until after I've looked over those printouts myself. Be that as it may, whatever Leon is up to, it can't be to our benefit. That the lizards have a crivit ranch at all is bad enough, without regard to what they intend it for."

"I agree," Mark said. "Even if our interpretation is wrong, I'd like to spoil their project. And I don't think we need to worry about Leon missing one of his animals. He'll just think it was a weakling the others killed off."

"His success is working in our favor," Arnold agreed. He looked up over Mark's shoulder, and the two computer scientists turned to see three people coming toward their table. One of the newcomers was Penny Carmichal. The other two were men in their middle forties, looking somehow out of place and uncomfortable in suits and ties.

Mark and Arnold rose to greet the newcomers, whom Penny introduced as Jack Corey and Wendel Fenister.

"We had a little trouble at the checkpoint," she said, "trying to get the lizards to believe we'd be interviewing animal handlers at this time of night, but the guards were pretty ignorant, and we threw jargon at them until they got tired and let us through."

"I just explained to them," Jack Corey said with a broad grin, "that you can't do anything with laboratory pigs during the day, at least not until they get to know you."

"Those guys must be late for their supper," Wendel Fenister said, "because they thought we meant guinea pigs, and their mouths started watering. That's what they didn't buy, since they know guinea pigs, but this lizard had never seen a real pig, and we spent a good while describing one to him. Got into razorbacks and black boars too. Pretended the lab pigs were like those instead of like farm breeds."

"It was really rather fun," Penny said.

"You gentlemen want any coffee, doughnuts while we talk?"

"You got any milk?" Corey asked as he and Fenister pulled chairs up to the table.

"Sure." Arnold went off to get it while Penny explained what was going on to Mark and Anne.

"Jack and Wendel," she said, "are going to get us our crivit."

"We're going to try anyway," Fenister said. "Jack's caught big cats, and he thinks he might have a way to do it."

"That's catfish," Corey said, responding to Mark's questioning glance. "Biggest one I ever caught weighed over two hundred pounds, a real monster."

"You mean you're going to *fish* for crivits?" Anne asked as Arnold came back with Corey's milk and a fresh cup of coffee.

"Makes sense, don't it?" Corey responded. "You can't shoot through sand any better than you can through water, and you can't get an animal like that to come up out into the air to get into a trap."

"Who-all's going on this expedition?" Mark asked.

"Just me," Arnold said. "If the three of us can't handle one crivit, then it's too big to bring in at all."

"Besides," Penny went on, "we don't want to attract too much attention. The fewer people involved, the more likely we are to go unnoticed by the lizards."

"It sounds," Anne said, "like you've already gotten it figured out. Why the meeting here tonight?"

"To figure out what kind of equipment we'll need," Corey said, "and what Arnold here can supply. It gets kind of inconvenient trying to talk about it on the phone without ever actually saying what you mean."

"We actually figured most of the stuff out on the way over here," Fenister said. "Goddamn, when Miss Carmichal told us what we were going after, I couldn't believe her at first. I mean, a monster that burrows in the sand?"

"At first," Corey said, "I thought she was talking about something like a badger or an armadillo."

"Sure is going to be a different kind of sport," Fenister agreed. "How long is it going to take us to get there tomorrow?" he asked, turning to Arnold.

"Less than an hour," Arnold said. "The site's in an area called the sand fields, down in Churchill County. You familiar with the area?"

"Hell, yes," Fenister said. "Right next to Durk Attweiler's farm."

"That's where we're going," Arnold said.

"Goddamn, that's all Durk needs, is monsters in his backyard. He know about this?"

"He showed me a crivit taking a pig last week."

"She-it," Corey said. "I guess our story about handling pigs had some truth to it after all."

"Ironically, yes," Arnold said. "We'll be taking one down with us tomorrow afternoon. But right now, let's go take a look at the equipment and decide what we need."

"We may have to jury-rig some stuff," Fenister said as he and Corey got to their feet.

"We've got a shop," Arnold said, following suit. He turned back to the others. "We'll see you later then," he said, then he and the two hunters left.

*   *   *

"There are some interesting implications in those transcripts you sent us last night," Penny said to Mark and Anne after Arnold and the hunters had left. "One report told about going for crivits for the breeding stock, and another one reported that they had been brought in. The two were just two hours apart, if your clock monitor can be trusted."

"An hour's flight by skyfighter can cover a pretty large area," Anne said.

"True," Penny agreed, "but if you consider the time it would take to load eight or so large carnivores, even if they cooperated, then you have a flight time one way of probably less than fifteen minutes."

"That does narrow the area considerably," Mark said. "And I think I see your point. Except for this one research station, the only place the Visitors keep crivits is guarding a prison camp."

"Right," Penny said. "And I didn't know there was a prison camp within fifteen minutes' flight of the RTP."

"Neither did I," Anne said. "And you know, that's just the kind of intelligence we've been hoping to uncover with our bugs at the Visitor headquarters. We've assumed that the people the Visitors have taken into custody were sent off to someplace like Florida or Mississippi."

"Looks like we get to do another global search tonight," Mark said. "I'll bet there have been references to this hypothetical camp that we just never recognized."

"And if you find it," Penny said, "then what? Help people escape?"

"That's a possibility," Mark said, "though not likely, since we're not equipped to do a job like that and it could jeopardize our own security. But if there's a secret camp here, then we might have a better chance of locating certain people who have just disappeared."

"Whatever we do or don't do," Anne said, "the more we know the better."

"We'll learn an awful lot more when the crivit comes

tomorrow," Penny said. "Speaking of which, I'd better find
Arnold and the others. I have to drive Corey and Fenister
back to Corey's place when they're through."

"All right then," Anne said as they all got up to leave.
"Let us know tomorrow how it comes out."

It was nearly eleven that night when Durk Attweiler
finally made up his mind to do a little "hunting." He'd
thought about it on and off all day long, but the prospect of
spying on the Visitors had daunted even him.

But he knew that the people he'd shown the crivit to
would be back, and when they came, there would be plenty
of risk without compounding it by being ignorant of the
extent of the Visitors' activities. Besides, he was curious.

He kept his anxiety over what he was to do under control
by not thinking about it. Instead he just acted. And the first
thing he did was to get down his shotgun and select shells
suitable for rabbits or squirrels. It had been a long time
since he'd done any midnight poaching, but that would be a
good excuse for being out if anybody caught him.

Then he opened a cabinet in his kitchen and moved
several canisters aside so he could reach the pint jars in
which he kept his personal stock of his last batch of
moonshine. Just one little sip, he said, to calm his nerves.
Then he smiled to himself and poured more of the potent
spirits into a smaller bottle he could easily slip into his
jacket pocket. Just as a kind of insurance, he told himself.

Leaving the lights on, he left the house. He didn't intend
to meet anybody, human or alien, while he was out, but if
he did, it would be better if he didn't have to try to explain
why he had snuck out. Lights on would look either like he
was still at home, or intending to be out only a short time.
Precautions like that came naturally to someone who ran an
illegal still.

He left the farmyard and walked through a soybean field
to his eastern fence line, and on north along it to where the
forest on the other side was densest. He'd seen a squirrel

nest somewhere around here, but in the dark it took him a moment to find it. It was not his practice to bag squirrels in their nest, but he knew other people who did. Besides, that was why he had come out, wasn't it? Just in case somebody should ask.

The first shot, nerve-rackingly loud in the stillness of the night, tore the nest apart. He heard two small thuds coming from under the tree where the nest had been and went to retrieve whatever had been there.

Both squirrels were still alive, and thrashing weakly, which enabled him to find them in the almost absolute blackness at the edge of the forest. Quickly he broke their necks and tied them by their hind legs to his belt with a bit of string. Hell, he might even get a good meal out of this expedition.

That done, he stood there for a long moment, listening to hear if anybody had been aroused by his shot and was coming to investigate. After fifteen minutes, with no sign of an investigation, he moved on. He went north to where he could go through the fence easily, and cut across Thurston's property toward the sand fields.

The forest was dark, but the sand fields, being without much in the way of trees or overhead foliage, were dimly lit from the sky. It was enough for him to find his way around the edge of the sand fields as he walked back toward Thurston's house toward the south.

He was more nervous being this close to where the crivits lived than he was at trespassing on Visitor property. Every little sound coming from the sand fields made him think that maybe one of the crivits was on his trail. He tried to reassure himself that as long as the ground underfoot was firm clay, the sand monsters couldn't get to him, but that didn't make him any the less jumpy.

Though he had not made it a habit of trespassing on Thurston's property in the past, he still had a general idea of the shape and extent of the sand fields. So it was with some surprise that he suddenly found himself walking on soft sand where there should have been hard clay. In a near panic he scrambled backward to more secure footing, and paused, panting, to hear if any crivits had detected him.

Apparently they hadn't. He knelt on the ground to see what he had walked into, and discovered that the soil bore the marks of large tires. This close to the ground it was also possible now to see that there were no plants at all in this disturbed area.

He moved forward carefully until he was right on the edge of the sand. With his imagination providing a crivit just out of sight, waiting to reach out and grab him, he felt with his hands until the nature of the soil suddenly came clear to him. This was not the natural sand of the area, contaminated with clay, gravel, rocks, and organic matter. This was pure quartz sand.

He looked down the line of the new sand, toward the Thurston house to the south. From here, he could see that a track had been cleared through the scraggly trees. In the darkness, it appeared to be about ten or twelve feet across, wide enough to serve as a road except for its surface. No one would pave a road with sand.

But if this was just the surface of a trench filled with sand, then it made sense. A road not for human or alien vehicles, but for sand-burrowing crivits.

He got to his feet and dusted off his knees. Now that he knew what he was looking at, he could see it more clearly, in spite of the darkness. He followed the crivit trench toward the Thurston house, staying a good two yards from the edge, just in case crivits could in fact reach that far out.

The question of what had been done with the soil that had been removed to make the trench was answered when he got to what he felt should be the back side of the Thurston farmyard, maybe a quarter mile from the house. Here the thick, dense red clay had been piled to one side, where there were no trees to interfere with the actions of the earth-moving equipment. He walked around the far side of the pile, away from the trench, trying to get a better view of what lay beyond. He did not want to climb the pile, since his footprints would give away the fact that he had been there, and once that was known, he was sure the lizards would come looking for him.

He heard the sounds of movement before he saw the lights, and stepped back into the deeper shadows under the trees. From here, his perspective allowed him to see a bit more of the farmyard beyond the mounds of clay soil, where lights from the house and one of the barns shone into the night. He listened to the sounds and decided that several of the Visitors were carrying something to the now invisible end of the sand trench.

Keeping to the trees, he moved around to the side to better see what was going on. The grove ended a little way farther on, and unless he wanted to expose himself against the western horizon, he could go no farther. The mounds of clay still concealed most of the action, but from this new point he could see that a chain-link fence had been erected, enclosing an area of about a quarter acre.

Within the fenced area were a few solitary trees and what had once been an abandoned meadow. The trees now looked oddly damaged, and the meadow, instead of being of a nearly uniform height, had places where the grasses and wild flowers appeared to have been mowed, random swaths cut through the green.

Two Visitors, their red uniforms almost black in the night, stood in the middle of the fenced area. One of them appeared to be holding some kind of animal, about the size of a large cat or a small dog. Durk heard a few muttered words, and then the Visitor threw the animal into the air, as if tossing it over a low fence. Then they both turned away, knelt to something that Durk could not see beause of the knee-high plants, and he heard a metallic rattling. When they stood up again, one of them was holding another one of the small animals. It too was tossed through the air.

Then the two Visitors waited silently. Durk wished he could see better and started to move forward, in spite of the

risk of being caught, when suddenly there came a frantic
scream from somewhere just in front of the two Visitors.

"Got one," Durk heard a male voice distinctly say. And
at the same time, the meadow and the branches of the few
solitary trees moved, as if other animals in them had taken
fright.

"Got the other," a female voice said, and now Durk
understood what he had been witnessing. The sand trench
led to the place just beyond where the two Visitors were
standing, and they had tossed the animals into the sand to
feed one of the crivits. Whatever the feed animals were,
there were obviously others in the area, which had reacted
with instinctual panic when the first of their number had
been taken.

"Hold on," a third voice, another male, said, calling
from somewhere behind the mounds of clay. "Okay, winch
it in."

The two Visitors Durk could see turned away from the
baiting and went to a shadowed shape he'd noticed but
hadn't been able to make out before. A moment later the
sound of a winch coming to life came to him. One of the
two Visitors stayed at the bulky shape of the winch while
the other disappeared behind it for a moment, then came
back pushing what looked like a hand cart of some kind.
The third Visitor came into view, skirting the far edge of
what must have been the fenced-in baiting area.

After a while the one at the winch turned it off, and the
other two moved the cart close to the short, invisible fence.
Moving as if they were unlocking a gate, they fiddled a
moment, then did something with the hand cart. The winch
whined for a moment, and Durk was just able to see the top
of a heavy wire cage rising up as if being dragged up a slope
toward them. It leveled off, the winch stopped, they
unhooked the cable, then closed the gate.

While the Visitor at the winch wound up the rest of the
cable, the other two pulled on the hand cart, dragging it
away toward the farmhouse. Durk knew what was inside the

cage, but was also sure he was glad he couldn't see it. They'd removed a crivit from its natural environment, for what purpose he couldn't guess and didn't want to know.

But the people up at the Research Triangle Park would want to know. He'd get hold of them tomorrow, one way or another. Right now, the thought of the raw whiskey in his bottle seemed more interesting. But not here, he thought. Carefully, he made his way back around the clay piles to the trench, and from there to the sand fields.

He was still a hundred feet or so from the fence when a bright light probed through the woods in his direction. This was what he had prepared for. Quickly, he took out his bottle of shine and drank off as much as he could at one gulp without choking. Then, holding the bottle in his right hand, and carrying his shotgun in the crook of his left elbow, he continued walking toward his fence.

"Hold it right there," a woman's voice called out. Its alien resonance was unmistakable.

"Wha?" he called back, and turned to face the light which had not yet caught him. "Whassa matter?" He deliberately thickened his speech and made himself weave slightly where he stood. The spotlight, aiming for the sound of his voice, at last found him. He shielded his eyes with his right arm, sloshing a bit of the moonshine over himself in the process.

"Put down that gun," the female alien called, coming nearer. Durk couldn't see her at all; the light was blinding him. "What are you doing here?" she went on as Durk carefully bent to lay his shotgun on the ground.

"Jus' doing a little squirrel hunting," he called back, making a visible effort to control his fictitious drunkenness. It wouldn't be all that fictitious in a moment or two.

"At night?" the Visitor asked sarcastically. She was within ten feet of him now, but he still couldn't see her other than as a vague shadow behind the brilliance of her light.

"Sure," he said, and reached down to his waist with his left hand.

"Be careful," the alien said in a tone of voice that Durk knew was serious. He jerked his hand away, then turned his left side toward the light so she could see the two squirrels dangling from his belt.

"You catch them in their nests at night," he said. Then he took a sip from his bottle.

"What's that?" the Visitor asked.

"Whiskey," Durk answered. He held out the bottle. "Want some?" She came up to him, took the bottle, sniffed its mouth.

"Gakhh," she said, handing it back. "How can you drink that stuff?"

"It's cheap," he said. He did not try to slur his voice now; the moonshine was providing enough of a slur by itself.

"Let me see those squirrels," the woman demanded. Durk fumbled with the string holding the animals to his belt a moment, sloshed moonshine, paused to put the cap back on, and put the bottle in his pocket, then managed to release his game and hold it out to her. She took the bodies, held them a moment.

"They're cold," she said.

"Been dead twenty minutes or more," he told her.

"How come I didn't hear any shooting?"

"I have no idea, lady. You want to take those squirrels home and do an autopsy?" He breathed heavily in her direction.

"No," she said and handed the animals back. "But I think you'd better be more careful about where you go hunting. These woods aren't safe, you know."

"Hell, hasn't been a bear anywhere around here in fifteen years."

"That's as may be," the woman said, and Durk could almost hear her smile, "but I'm here now, and so are other Visitors, and we're a match for any bear."

"Ah, right."

"Now pick up your rifle and go."

"Yes, ma'am," Durk said. Moving slowly, he retrieved his shotgun, and walked unsteadily toward the fence. The Visitor followed him and watched him climb unsteadily over.

"When we catch people trespassing," she said as he started to walk away, "we don't turn them over to the sheriff." He stopped to look back over his shoulder at where she stood in the darkness. "Get my meaning?" she asked.

"I do," he said, then turned and walked away.

Chapter 6

As Professor Morton Barnes was unlocking his office door the next morning, Alice Marshall, the secretary he shared with the others on the third floor, came out into the hall to speak with him.

"I just thought you'd like to know," she said. "We found out who those students were who got arrested after trashing the Visitor liaison office."

"Ah," Barnes said, pausing with his key still in the lock. "Anyone I know?"

"David Androvich was one of them," Alice said.

"Damn," Morton said, opening the door the rest of the way. "He was a good student. Had a real knack for math. Have his parents been informed?"

"Yes, and the others too."

"All right, I'll make a note in his file. Thank you."

He went in and sat down at his desk, but the news bothered him more than he thought it would. Compounded with his anxiety for his own safety, it left him completely unable to get to work on the papers that still needed grading.

Instead, he pulled out the grade book for the class in which Androvich was enrolled and made a note in the margin that the boy was "unofficially withdrawn, without penalty." After all, it wasn't Dave's fault that he'd been taken away.

Except of course that it was. If he'd attended to his

studies and not tried to act against the Visitors in so foolish a way, he'd still be free.

Morton thought about Kenny Borgman's brief but frightening letter about his experiences in the Visitor prison camp, and about Dave and his friends now suffering the same fate. He wished there were something he could do, and even as he did so he realized that it was the same wish, basically, that had caused those students to do what they did, however misguided they had been.

But from all he'd heard so far, Dave and his friends had accomplished no more than to cause the Visitors a minor inconvenience. Surely they didn't deserve to be turned into slaves just for that. Or worse. Besides, they were so young.

At last he couldn't stand it anymore. He left his office and the Smythe Building, and walked down the quad to the Visitor liaison offices in Courtland. There he asked to see Jozef, the Visitor campus liaison, and after a moment's wait, was shown into the office.

If this was where the students had done their vandalism, there was no sign of it now. Jozef, a spare man who assumed the appearance of one in his late forties in part, Morton was sure, to enhance his aura of authority, stood up to greet him.

"What can I do for you, Professor Barnes?" he asked, not uncordially.

"I know it's none of my business," Morton started hesitantly, "but one of the boys who was responsible for the vandalism to your offices here has been a student of mine for over three years."

"I see. That certainly explains your interest, but as you said, his fate is not your business."

"I know that, but you do understand that it pains me to think about what will happen to him. And to the others too, of course. That their action was criminal cannot be denied, nor the fact that they should be punished. But I couldn't in good conscience fail to take the opportunity to ask you to remember that they are, after all, little more than children."

"College seniors are not children, Professor Barnes, as I'm sure they will remind you themselves."

"But doesn't the very stupidity of what they did prove that they are nonetheless not yet adults?"

"Perhaps, but I don't see what that has to do with anything."

"It means that you might treat them with more clemency than you would a hardened rebel."

"It is such amateurs as these," Jozef said, "that eventually turn into 'hardened rebels,' as you call them. It is far better to stop them early, before they can do real damage, and before they pervert others to their distorted way of thinking."

"But surely, they did you no real harm. Is it necessary to send them away to a prison camp somewhere? Couldn't you let us try them in our own courts?"

"Their crime was serious by intent, if not by accomplishment. And it was against us, not against you. If other students vandalize your office, Professor Barnes, we shall not interfere and let you deal with them in your own way."

"How long will you keep them?" Barnes asked, beginning to feel it had been a mistake to come here.

"I cannot tell you that, and if I could, I wouldn't. I'm sorry, Professor Barnes, I wish I could reassure you, but it would be false of me to try to do so. As you said at the very beginning, this is no business of yours."

"All right." He turned heavily toward the door. "Thank you for listening to me anyway."

"It's my job," Jozef said, and watched the man leave, his shoulders sagging.

Jozef sat there for a long moment, thinking about what Barnes had said. He was not the first to have come and ask about those five students, and he would not be the last. That these people showed concern for and interest in the vandals was only natural. He would have done the same had the positions been reversed.

But he dared not tell any of them what was in store for the vandals, though he disapproved of part of it himself. The situation was uncomfortable enough as it was, without these people—a subject people, though they didn't fully realize it yet—knowing that those prisoners who could not be made use of would wind up as a gourmet feast for those who had acquired the taste for human flesh. No, that knowledge would make the whole situation altogether untenable.

Something was still bothering him. He had been so concerned about being noncommittal that he had missed the import of some of Barnes's words. What was it—ah, yes, prison camp. Now how had Barnes known about a prison camp? No other human who had talked to him so far had mentioned such a thing—prison, yes, or execution once, but not camp.

Such a little thing, and yet not a part of this people's general conception of what was done to prisoners. A tiny slip, but it could indicate that Barnes in fact knew a little more than he should. He reached out, touched the communicator, and spoke into it.

"Chang," he said, "Jozef here. We may be in for some more trouble on campus. At least one person had mentioned 'prison camp' to me in a way that indicates he has some idea of what he's talking about."

"Let's not be hasty," Chang said, the speaker emphasizing rather than diminishing the resonant quality of her alien voice. "But perhaps you'd better keep an eye on this person, just in case. Camp T-3 is not yet that secure, and though we have no known rebel activity in the area, knowledge of its existence could be just enough to produce it."

"Very good," Jozef said. "I'll hold back, but I'll start a quiet investigation right away."

Under normal circumstances, Durk found cultivating his bean fields an undemanding, quietly satisfying, and relaxing chore. Of course, when the tractor broke down or the cultivator hung up on a rock, it became less pleasant. But today it was different. Today, as never before, he was aware of the sandy quality of the soil. And "sandy" had taken on a whole new meaning for him lately, aside from its implications of low fertility and production.

The bean fields were quite a way south from the place on the Thurston farm—he'd better start thinking of it as the Visitors' farm, he thought—where the crivits were kept. And the soil here was nowhere as loose as in the sand fields, but it was not as firm as he'd like it. It made him nervous, just thinking about those monsters, whatever they were, being able to burrow away from their captivity onto his own farm.

His nervousness changed to complete alarm when, working his way eastward, he noticed what looked like mole-runs in the soil. Two things marked them as distinct, however. They avoided the plants, instead of running from one to another, and they were fully two feet wide. He stopped his tractor before the front wheels could cross over the nearest track.

The situation, he thought, was quickly getting out of hand. He didn't like the Visitors, didn't want them as his neighbors, but he could live with that if they kept to themselves. He had decided, after his "squirrel hunt" encounter with them, to stay clear of the Visitors altogether and to not go up to the Research Triangle Park after all. Whatever those scientists wanted to do, it could only get him into trouble.

But now, here was evidence that made it difficult to ignore what was going on in the next farm. Even if he never trespassed on their property again, even if he averted his eyes whenever he had to drive by, he was not going to be left alone.

He got down off his tractor and walked slowly and carefully to the slightly mounded track just five feet in front of the front wheels. Just exactly like a mole burrow, he thought. He couldn't tell when it had been made; it could have been this morning or more than a week ago. He knelt at the track and picked at the upthrust soil.

Surface cracks were dry all the way down, but there had been no rain recently, so that meant only that it had been made since the last rain, and he'd been over this field once since then. He stood up and kicked at the disturbed soil with his boot. A small section of the mound collapsed, sinking several inches below the level of the field.

He didn't want to do this, a part of his mind yammered as he kicked away more of the soil to reveal a half-filled hollow underneath the mound. He reached down, on his knees, and cleared away the fallen earth with his hands. The hole revealed was a lot bigger than the track on the surface indicated, maybe eighteen inches across, its roof a foot under the top of the mound. It was almost big enough for a man to crawl into.

That thought got him up on his feet in a hurry. He tried to imagine a creature eighteen inches in diameter and strong enough to make a tunnel like that in this ground, and he couldn't. Where did it keep its tentacles? How did it know where it was going? He had no answers.

More importantly, why was it here at all? From what he had seen before, the monsters preferred to burrow deeply, except when they were hunting. This track was just below the surface, for as much of it as he could see. The subsoil, he knew, was far harder than that on the surface, and even that was made dense by clay, moisture, and organic matter.

He didn't know in which direction the creature had been moving, but guessed that it had come from the north. He followed the track in that direction, all too painfully aware of the sandy nature of the ground on which he walked. Had the thing been hungry? Had it just been curious about a break in its natural perimeter, come out for a look around, and gotten lost? Had some animal, such as a deer or a possum or even a dog come by its preserve and run away, drawing it out into less congenial territory?

The track, when it had to pass under a row of beans, did so with a sharp S-curve. Otherwise, it stayed between the rows, giving it an artificially linear formation. Had the rows not been there, he realized after crossing over the same one three times, the creature probably would have just gone around in circles. He had no doubt that it had come up from the area near where he had showed those scientists how it could take a pig right down into the sand. It was more important, he realized, to figure out where it had wound up.

He turned around and started back toward his tractor, surprised that he had come so far from it. He didn't bother following the crivit track, but took the most direct route. One thing was sure: he was not going to continue cultivating this field. Even if the monster had found its way home, the tunnels it had left would collapse under the weight of the tractor's front wheels, causing it to pitch forward and certainly bogging it down. Then he'd have to bring his truck out to haul the tractor out, and that would destroy a portion of his crop. No, further cultivation could wait until later, after he'd gone through with a shovel and knocked all the burrows flat, maybe even filled in some of them to make the ground level again.

His concern with the immediate and practical consequences of this invasion so occupied him that he was halfway back to his tractor before he became aware of the sound that had begun when he'd turned away from the source of the burrows. Something like cement sliding down a cement truck's chute, something like the movement of rocks underwater, it had grown steadily louder until at last it penetrated his consciousness. He froze for a moment, listening.

And even as he did so he knew he should be running instead. Though he'd never heard a sound exactly like that before, he knew without doubt what it was—a crivit coming through the soil.

It was coming from ahead of him, from beyond the tractor, but not in the row in which he was now standing. It grew louder, but he had no idea how near it was, had no way to gauge its speed of approach. The tractor, idling just two hundred feet away, made less noise than the thing did.

He took a step, then saw, two rows over, the tops of bean plants just fifty feet away rise up a few inches. A few seconds later and the next row did a similar lift.

And then he saw it—a mound in the soil moving toward

him at a rate that seemed phenomenal. He made a small sound in his throat, remembered once seeing a cotton rat standing frozen as a blacksnake approached, and then he broke, turned, and ran across the field, trampling rows of beans as he crossed them. He couldn't help himself; he had to look over his shoulder, and the moving mound, with loose dirt flying into the air, was right behind him, not ten feet back. He put his head down and ran as hard as he could.

When the soil firmed unexpectedly under his feet he staggered, managed a few paces more, then fell headlong across a row of beans. With a cry he forced himself to his feet, looking once again over his shoulder, but there was no sign of pursuit behind him. Of course, coming across the rows, he wouldn't see it until it was right on him. He scanned the bean field, looking for the telltale rise of the tops of the plants. There was nothing.

His tractor was back there, idling away until its fuel would run out. He didn't care. He walked, quickly, still farther from the sandy area, trying to catch his breath, trying to listen for the telltale sound of the crivit approaching. He eventually succeeded in the former and was equally if not more pleased in failing in the latter endeavor. Staying on ground that he knew was too dense with clay to permit even a mole, let alone a crivit, he worked his way back to his house.

Still mulling over this morning's interview with Jozef, Morton Barnes walked back from lunch at the Porthole Restaurant, halfway planning to contact Dave Androvich's parents.

As he walked past the cars filling the Smythe Building parking lot, he noticed a red-uniformed Visitor standing beside the Evergreen House. The woman pretended to be looking the other way, but Barnes was not fooled.

As he mounted the steps at the north entrance to Smythe, he pretended to drop the book he was carrying, and when he bent to pick it up took the opportunity to pause and look back the way he had come. The Visitor was still there,

rapidly turning away so as not to be seen watching him.
Barnes felt the lunch in his stomach grow hard and
indigestible. It had, indeed, been a mistake to go talk to
Jozef.

He entered the foyer and walked down the hall to the
central lobby with the stairs going up. The door on the other
side of the lobby closed, but not before he caught the merest
glimpse of red. Of course, red was a popular color, and
many students, and even faculty, wore red on occasion.

But not of that particular shade. Only Visitors now wore
that red. He went up the stairs to the third floor, and instead
of thinking about calling Androvich's parents, started
thinking about calling his own family—to say good-bye.

He paused at the top of the stairs and looked down both
ends of the corridor. He saw no Visitors, but that didn't
mean anything. He stopped in at the secretary's office and
asked if there were any messages. There were none. More
importantly, her behavior indicated that nothing untoward
had happened since he'd left—such as Visitors come
calling.

But that didn't mean that nobody had been there. He let
himself into his office, thinking that with classes and lunch,
it had been three hours since he'd been here. He sat down at
his desk and forced himself to relax, letting his eyes go
around the room, looking for signs that it wasn't as it had
been three hours ago.

He saw nothing out of place, but was not reassured. He
reached for his phone and picked it up. But even as he
brought the handset up to his face, he smelled something,
like slightly charred electrical insulation. Sniffing, he
identified the source as coming from the phone's mouth-
piece. There were no wires extending from it, but he put it
down nonetheless. It had not smelled that way earlier this
morning. Maybe it was just a short—but he didn't believe
that.

He spent a few moments idly flipping through the papers
on his desk, more to pass the time than to take note of what
he was looking at. Then he pushed his chair back, went to

his filing cabinet, pawed aimlessly through a drawer for a moment, and came back to the window behind his desk to look out.

And to look up and down the frame, behind the blinds, out at the bricks of the outside wall. Nothing seemed out of place. He turned and looked at his desk.

He went to his knees and, without making a sound, moved so that he could see into the kneehole. There, at the back, was a tiny black disk which he knew had not been there before.

Now that he knew, much of his anxiety left him. His office was bugged, and he knew very well that it was the Visitors, probably at Jozef's instructions, who had done it. He sat back in his chair and started going over the stack of papers. It was amazing, he thought, how he could return to his work with such concentration while at the same time he was screaming inside.

By the time he reached his house, Durk's panic had subsided and had been replaced by a grim determination. He couldn't work without his tractor, and he could hear the crivits coming, and the soil around the tractor was dense enough that he could outrun the monsters, so he had decided that he would go back and get his tractor.

But not without his shotgun. He went in the back door and pulled open the cabinet in the back hall where he kept his spare ammunition. There were still ten buckshot shells, heavy enough to stop anything except a bear, and even a bear would slow down a minute when hit. He grabbed three—more would be superfluous, and went into his living room.

As he did so he heard a car drive up. He ignored it, took down his shotgun, and, taking out the squirrel shot, loaded it with the heavier ammunition. His front door reverberated with a heavy knocking.

He went to the door, gun in hand as if he might be expecting trouble—which he was. When he opened the door, he found Wendel Fenister, Arnold Rutgers, and another man standing on his front porch.

"How you doin', Durk?" Wendel asked, eyeing the shotgun.

"Not bad," Durk said, looking from the hunter to the scientist to the other man. "Afternoon, Mr. Rutgers. I guess this isn't just a social call."

"I'm afraid not," Rutgers said. "Can we come in?"

"Sure, this gun's not for you." Durk stood aside and let the three men into his living room. "Thought about calling you up this morning," he said to Arnold, "then changed my mind. Maybe it's just as well you stopped by." He then told them of his spying trip of the night before, and of the crivit tracks out by his abandoned tractor.

"If it's still out there," Arnold said, "we'd like to go take a look. You know Wendel Fenister, of course. This is Jack Corey. He's got a plan to catch one of those monsters, and I don't suppose you'd mind it being gone from your field." He looked significantly at the shotgun Durk was still carrying.

"How are you going to catch something like that?" Durk asked.

"Like fishing for catfish," Corey said. "We've got a pig for bait, a harness full of hooks, and a steel cable on a winch in the back of the truck."

"You got this thing all figured out, don't you?" Durk said with a hint of admiration in his voice. "But what's your cover if the lizards come by?"

"You've provided us with one," Arnold said. "You're tractor's broken down, and we've come to help you tow it back to the barn."

"That'll do," Durk said. "I don't think those lizards over there are smart enough to figure out I could do it myself. They bought my squirrel-hunting story last night. All right, let's go give it a try."

Durk, sitting next to Arnold in the driver's seat while the other two rode in the back of the truck, directed the scientist up the west side of his property, taking the long way around to stay clear of the more sandy soil for as long as possible. When they came to a line between sections, Arnold turned back east again, rolling over ground that owed its poor fertility to quartz rock rather than sand. Arnold slowed when they came within sight of the tractor.

"I've got to get close enough to use the winch," Arnold said.

"All right," Durk said. "Turn around and back up. I'll guide you in." He got out of the truck and met Corey and Fenister getting off the back.

"Can that thing actually move through soil like this?" Corey asked, kicking at the clay.

"Not here, I don't think," Durk said. "It gets a lot looser toward the tractor." He and the two hunters started walking toward it as Arnold turned the truck around so that it could back in and bring the winch to bear.

They had gone only a little ways when Arnold started honking at them.

"What is it?" Durk called.

"I don't want to mess up your beans. Which way should I go?"

"Screw the beans—just follow me." He waited until Arnold had backed the truck up almost to where he was standing before starting out again.

Corey and Fenister were quite a way ahead. "Watch your feet," Durk called to them. "You can outrun it, but no sense drawing the thing here until you've got your bait ready." The two hunters halted where they stood.

Durk knew this ground like he knew the top of his dining room table. He did not go straight to the tractor, but arched around to the left and north, directing the truck over the harder soil. Corey and Fenister, realizing what he was doing, came back to join him.

"Is that the track?" Fenister said, pointing to a place where the ground was heaved up in a long, narrow pile.

"Sure is," Durk said. "Wasn't there before. Look, the ground's too hard, see how it keeps trying to come this way and then turning back? Four rows farther on, there's lots of sand. I think we'll be safe right here."

He signaled to Arnold to stop the truck. They were still a little west and somewhat north of the tractor, and saw its exhaust flap bounce up and down as it idled. Durk went up to the truck to talk with Arnold.

"How much cable you got?" he asked.

"A thousand feet," Arnold said. "Is that enough?"

"Should be. Let's get your pig ready."

"I'd like to look at those burrows first."

"You look at them with the pig ready, the crivit will know we're out there and it will come for us. If we don't have the pig, we won't be able to take it back as bait without being caught ourselves."

"All right then," Arnold said and got out of the truck. He left the motor running. Corey and Fenister came up, and together they set to work.

The winch was in the back of the truck bed, right up against the cab, with a boom which held the cable out of the way of the tailgate. In front of the winch were two cages, the smaller one holding a sixty-pound pig, the larger one empty. Arnold and the hunters were hoping to take the monster alive, but Durk kept his shotgun handy.

Corey and Fenister got the pig out of its cage and held it steady while Arnold got the harness on it. This was made of heavy leather straps that went over the pig's shoulders, around its body at the middle, and under its stomach just in front of its back legs. There was a snap hook on top between the pig's shoulders, and a dozen six-inch hooks mounted on swivels on the top, sides, and bottom of the harness. The swivels were such that, from whatever direction the monster took the pig, the hooks would bite.

"Pig doesn't seem afraid," Wendel Fenister commented as Arnold finished fastening the buckles.

"It's sedated," Arnold said. "We used a new tranquilizer that calms you down without putting you to sleep."

Carefully, now that the pig was "armed," they carried it down out of the truck. Arnold went back, threw a lever on the winch, and drew out enough cable so that it could be hooked to the pig's harness. Then he took two leather straps, each about eight feet long, and fastened them to the harness as well. Corey and Fenister each took a strap and, standing on either side of the pig, were able to make it walk between them.

"That sure is fancy," Durk said when they were finished. "Now let's go look at the crivit burrow."

They walked through the beans toward the sandier ground, the cable trailing behind them from the now free-running winch. When they came to the first of the burrow mounds, they stopped.

"What's under there?" Arnold asked, indicating the burrow.

"Kick it in and look," Durk said. Arnold did so, revealing the hole through the soil below. The pig began to get nervous.

"It's big," Arnold said, kneeling down to clear away some dirt so he could look into the hole. He brushed his hand along the bottom of the burrow. "Heavier clay down here," he said. "That means it can't dive deeper like it did at the sand flats." Behind him, the pig began to squeal softly and jerk at its straps.

"Somebody," Fenister said, "doesn't like being used for bait."

"Can you smell anything down that hole?" Corey asked.

Arnold lowered his head and sniffed. "Just clay and dirt," he said, his nose wrinkling. "Anaerobic bacteria. If the crivit left a scent, I can't detect it."

"The pig sure can," Fenister said. He and Corey had a firm grip on their straps, cinched up short to keep the pig with its deadly hooks from moving.

Arnold got to his feet. "This has got to be pretty nearly as far as the monster can go," he said. "Let's take the pig farther out."

The hunters dragged the pig toward the burrow and had to lift it into the air when they got to the mounded dirt. The pig, squealing and thrashing, tried to bite off the straps but couldn't quite reach them. Arnold stayed where he was, making sure the cable was clear, and Durk walked ahead of the hunters, testing the soil with his feet and listening hard for the telltale sound of an approaching crivit.

As they went farther into crivit territory, the pig stopped protesting and went rigid.

"It makes *me* frightened," Corey said, "watching that animal freeze like that."

"At least it won't run away when we put it down," Fenister said.

They crossed over another burrow and stopped at a third.

"How can you tell when it's coming?" Fenister asked as they set the pig on its feet. The animal stood there, trembling.

"You can hear it," Durk said. "It makes more noise than you might think when it moves through the ground."

"How about if it comes back through one of its old tunnels?" Corey asked.

"Then, uh . . ." Durk started to say and then he too froze. "Hush!" he hissed. "Then they make a lot less noise," he said, turning his head from side to side. "Goddamn, let's get out of here."

He started walking quickly back toward the truck. Corey and Fenister hesitated uncertainly for a moment, then started unwrapping the straps from their hands so they could let the pig go. And just a hundred feet from them, the burrow they were next to began to shift and settle, the movement coming toward them at a frightening rate.

"Get out of there," Durk called to the two hunters. "Set the winch," he yelled to Arnold, who didn't yet know what was going on. Corey and Fenister at last managed to drop the straps and started to back away from the pig when the burrow right in front of them burst open and two long, wrist-thick tentacles came up waving. In an instant the pig was wrapped in the sinuous appendages and dragged into the ground.

"Goddamn," Arnold said, and belatedly ran back to the truck. The cable was unreeling rapidly. Corey and Fenister stopped retreating and instead grabbed the cable, trying to slow it down.

"It's going to run the whole thing out," Corey yelled as Arnold sprinted the last few feet to the truck and grabbed for the winch controls. He threw on the brake, and the wire went taught. Then he engaged the gears and started winding the cable back in.

"We've got it," Fenister said, running down the burrow. The cable had sliced through the churned-up soil and now disappeared into the ground a hundred feet away. He grabbed the cable and gave it a jerk to try to set the hooks.

"Give me a hand," he called, and Corey started to go to him.

"Stay clear," Durk yelled. "If it lets go of the pig, it will snap out of the ground and hook *you*."

The sandy soil churned where the cable disappeared into the ground. Back at the truck, Arnold applied more power to the winch, and slowly the cable began to draw back. But only for a moment. The winch motor whined, the cable thrummed, but the crivit seemed to have gotten a grip in the earth and was not going to come out of the hole.

"I'll get shovels," Corey yelled, and started running back toward the truck.

"Damn fool," Durk said. He made sure his shotgun was loaded, then walked over to where Fenister was jerking on the cable, not ten feet from the churning soil through which, on occasion, a tentacle could be seen reaching up into the air.

"Get back," Durk called to Fenister. "It can reach you."

And just then the monster stopped pulling and surged forward, half out of the ground. The cable went slack for a moment, and the monster, only dimly perceived, flung its tentacles around Fenister's legs and dragged him off his feet.

Durk felt like he was moving in slow motion. He saw Fenister go down, saw a series of shorter tentacles reaching for the man's legs, saw what looked like a great parrot's beak opening, down which went the end of the cable. He strode as quickly as he could, only five paces off, and it seemed to take forever. He raised the shotgun, watched as Fenister's feet were grabbed by the shorter tentacles surrounding the beak, saw the beak close, shearing away part of Fenister's boot, and aimed the shotgun at a point on the monster's body just above its maw.

He fired, the animal thrashed, Fenister cried out. Durk stepped closer, looking for something like an eye or a head. The monster oozed green blood, thrashing and battering Fenister but not drawing him any nearer. Durk aimed right into the monster's mouth, just past Fenister's ankle, and fired again.

The tentacles, long and short, flailed, letting Fenister go. The monster started to back down into its burrow, throwing dirt forward as it did so. Its beak worked, and the cable started to fray. Moving like an automaton, Durk stepped up right on top of the thing. He had only one more shot. He couldn't see the creature for the soil, but he aimed at a spot about a foot behind the chomping beak and fired straight down.

He was thrown off his feet into a row of beans. Corey and Arnold were shouting from somewhere far off. Durk pulled himself to his knees, saw tentacles standing stiffly up into the air, contorted in painful knots and arches. And then they relaxed and drooped down to the ground.

Corey and Arnold came running up as he got to his feet. Fenister was pulling himself away from the monster with his hands. Corey dropped his shovel and knelt beside his friend.

"Are you all right?"

"Goddamn, nearly broke my leg," Fenister said. Corey looked down at his feet.

"Nearly bit your foot off too," he said. He helped Fenister get up.

"I thought it had me there for a while," Fenister said. His face was mottled red and white. "Goddamn."

"Let's get you back to the truck," Corey said. He

dropped his shovel and put his arm under Fenister's shoulders.

Meanwhile, Arnold was digging tentatively at the monster's head. Durk came up to him and looked down into the burrow.

"It nearly bit through your cable," he said, letting the barrel of the shotgun drag. Arnold looked up at him with frightened eyes.

"I—" he said, "I—"

Durk stepped over the burrow and grabbed the scientist's shoulder. He shook him, hard.

"It's dead now," Durk said. "Let's go back to the truck and pull it out with the winch."

"Goddamn," Arnold gasped. He stepped back, shook himself all over, and gradually regained his composure. He looked back at the burrow. "And we thought we were going to take it alive," he said.

Fenister was sitting on the tailgate when they got back to the truck.

"How you doing?" Durk asked the hunter.

"Nothing broken," Fenister said. "Nothing missing, except the sole of my boot." He held up his foot. Only a part of the toe of the sole was left. The sock was cut, but the skin was unbroken underneath.

"He's damned lucky," Corey said. "If I ever go fishing after one of those monsters again, I'm going to take a harpoon."

"Let's get this one out of here first," Durk said. He went to the winch and started the motor again. Slowly at first, and then more quickly the cable started winding up. The four men stood at the truck, watching the bean plants go down as the crivit was dragged across the field toward them.

Then Durk noticed other bean plants waving off to one side.

"We've got company," he said, pointing. Another two feet of beans in the next row nearer lifted up a couple of inches, then settled back down. "Can't hear it because of the winch," he said.

"Damn," Arnold said, putting more power into the winch. "Those things are cannibals." The winch groaned, the cable sang, and the dead crivit occasionally bounced into sight as it was dragged across the rows.

"Get him in the truck," Arnold said to Corey. "Durk, move that big cage out of the way. We're just going to drag the monster on and run."

Durk climbed into the back of the truck as Corey helped Fenister around to the passenger's side. There was nowhere to move the cage to, so he just threw it over the side of the bed, and then dumped the pig cage too. He reached for the boom and swung it to one side so that the crivit would come up right over the tailgate.

He could see it now, and could see the signs of three other crivits grinding through the soil toward it. But the soil was too heavy for the living monsters to make much speed. The dead creature was well in advance.

It was shaped roughly like a squid, but instead of smooth sides, it had lots of small tentacles which ended in flat digging feet. Besides the two long grabbing tentacles and the dozen or so smaller holding ones around its mouth, there were four or five broader diggers, now all hanging limply. The body looked to be about six feet long and was a grayish blue color without markings.

Arnold slowed the winch as the monster was dragged up to within feet of the truck, and Durk manipulated the boom to lift it off the ground. Quickly, they brought the thing onto the truck bed. Arnold went to get in behind the wheel, and Corey came back out to ride with Durk. When he saw the thing in the truck, he almost decided to walk.

"That one's no danger," Durk said, kicking the corpse. "Those are, though." He pointed to where giant mole mounds were slowly grinding through the dense soil toward the truck. Then Arnold put the truck into gear and they went off with a jerk.

Durk stood on his porch and watched the truck drive off with its bizarre cargo. Though just a short while ago he had decided to leave the Visitors to themselves, the crivit hunt had changed his mind again. He didn't know how far the remaining crivits might penetrate into his bean field, but he didn't care. Their being there at all was more than he could stand.

There was no sense now, he knew, in trying to go back for his tractor. At least three other crivits were at large, and though he could run faster than they could burrow through fresh soil, they could retrace their tracks quickly and almost silently. It would be just too dangerous.

Nor was there any sense in going over to his alien neighbors to complain. Not only would they not care about his troubles, they might even take that as a sign that he had become dangerous to them. And he was not in a position to go in and attack them single-handed.

He went back into his living room. He thought he might like a drink right about now, but he was almost out of moonshine. Better save what was left for a time when it might really be needed. Meanwhile, he could start thinking about making up another batch.

He found himself staring at a large, white rock sitting on a shelf in the corner case. It was just a piece of quartz, a mass of thumb-sized crystals clinging to a coarser matrix. Deep in the crevices between individual crystals were tiny flecks of gold. There wasn't enough of the precious metal there to fill a tooth, but it was a pretty rock, and it made him think about the mine from which it had come two generations ago.

The mining operation had not been very extensive, and most of it underlay Thurston's property, where the rock formations existed. But one tunnel had been driven under the Attweiler farm, with permission and the payment of a fee, to facilitate loading what ore there was into flat-bottomed boats riding the Saksapaw River.

The more he knew about the Visitors next door, the better. And the scientists up at the Research Triangle Park might be able to use that knowledge to counter what the Visitors were doing, or maybe even to drive them off.

He got a heavy flashlight, went back outside, got in his truck, and drove it over to the riverbank. The last twenty feet along the top of the bank were uncultivated and covered with bushes and trees. The bank itself was steep, the river rushing brown and dirty thirty feet below. Durk drove up to a place where the bank had fallen in a bit and parked his truck.

Climbing down the bank was not easy. It was a cliff of clay, steep, with few handholds, and the clay crumbled under his feet and hands. But he knew where he wanted to go. He'd discovered the place as a boy. When his father had found out where he'd been, he'd closed the old tunnel mouth up. But that was years ago, and the river had undercut the end of the tunnel. If he was lucky, it would have opened it up again.

He was lucky. The square, black mouth gaped in the side of the clay cliff, its floor only five feet up from the water. He snapped on the flashlight and peered into the tunnel. Part of the roof had collapsed here, but farther in, the tunnel was clear. With a grim smile, Durk stepped into the darkness.

Chapter 7

Bill Gray sat alone in the secret underground lab under Data Tronix. Around him, the dozens of monitor screens glowed, but most of them were blank. The computer-generated plans of the Visitor headquarters had long since been filled in as far as possible, and all the lines there that had been bugged had also been identified. Now it was a simple matter of monitoring those lines, recording unusual power usages, recording intercom and phone conversations, and pulling off everything that went through the alien computer buses for later analysis.

Bill's job, at the moment, was to listen in on external communications. Intercom messages would be recorded, transcribed automatically, and checked by others upstairs. But phone calls coming into or going out of the headquarters building were more important, and occasionally Bill would make special recordings for immediate analysis.

When Mark Casey came in to bring him a fresh thermos of coffee, Bill handed him a printout. "We recorded this this morning," Bill said, "but somehow it slipped our attention."

Mark put down the thermos and looked at the printout.

SPEAKER A: Chang, Jozef here. We may be in for some more trouble on campus. At least one person has mentioned "prison camp" to me in a way that indicates he has some idea of what he's talking about.

SPEAKER B: Let's not be hasty. But perhaps you'd better keep an eye on this person, just in case. Camp T-3 is not yet that secure, and though we have no known rebel activity in the area, knowledge of its existence could be just enough to produce it.

SPEAKER A: Very good. I'll hold back, but I'll start a quiet investigation right away.

"Very interesting," Mark said when he finished reading. "That confirms our suspicions all right."

"I think," Bill said, "that Camp T-3 is where they took those students."

"More than likely. I wish the hell we could do something about it."

"I've asked Shirley to come up with a special routine to analyze all headquarters-to-skyfighter communications. We know that wherever the camp is it's somewhere in the quadrant south of the RTP, since flights don't come over this way, and observers elsewhere are keeping track of air traffic. If she can come up with a way to get the range of a skyfighter from its signal strength, we may be able to pin down the camp's location a lot better."

"Now, that's good," Mark said. "At least it will confine it to an arc somewhere. But we need more observers. And the trouble is, without a history of strong rebel action here, there are few people who want to make the effort or take the chance."

"I guess you can't have it both ways. Either the lizards tromp all over you, like they did in Los Angeles or New York or Chicago and you develop a strong, active underground who you can call on later, or they more or less leave you alone, as they're doing here, and then you have nobody with rebel experience."

"To tell you the truth," Mark said, "I prefer it this way. Compared to some other places, we've had very few casualties and missing people."

"It may not keep on that way," Bill said, "if this camp of theirs gets into full swing."

* * *

The tunnel from the river to the old mine head was straight, though it was occasionally crossed by others. Durk Attweiler had no difficulty finding his way, though it had been more than twenty-five years since he had been here. One could get lost in the side passages, but this tunnel had been intended to get ore from the mine to the river by the quickest possible route.

He stood now at the bottom of a shaft, in which an elevator powered by mules above had once been suspended. That contrivance had long since collapsed, as had the protective shed atop the shaft. As he looked up, he could see only one or two dim sparks of light twenty feet overhead.

He played the flashlight around the sides of the shaft, looking for a way up. The ground was mostly rock here, with bits of quartz glinting in the flashlight's beam. There were no supporting timbers lining the walls of the shaft, but it was built square, and the surface was rough enough that he thought he could climb up one of the corners.

He turned off the flash, put it down to one side where he could find it again, and groped his way to the far corner of the shaft. Indeed, the rocky walls offered plenty of projections, and he got maybe six feet up before he ran into trouble. A stone came loose in his hand, and only by flattening himself into the corner did he save himself from a fall. But that convinced him that this was not the best way to get to the surface. His judgment was proved correct when he tried to come back down. Going up in the dark was one thing, coming down was another, and though the drop was a short one, the floor of the shaft was irregular, and broken stones and planks would make any fall hazardous.

When he finally regained the safety of the bottom, he recovered his flashlight and went back into the tunnel, looking for something with which to make a ladder. At this point, there were a number of large galleries, as well as more than a dozen side tunnels. The route to the river was plain, at least to his eyes, but beyond that he could easily get lost.

He found what he wanted in a side alcove that proved to be the top of another shaft leading down to lower levels. Access was by ladder, and though the wood was old, it had resisted rot and insect damage and seemed sound. He pulled the ladder up out of the hole, working backward to make it fit. Originally, it had probably been constructed in sections, and was so long that it took more than a little effort to twist it just the right way so that it would come free.

But free it came at last. He dragged and maneuvered it back to the mine head, and worked the top end up the shaft. It was four feet short, so he built a platform out of timber ends to raise the bottom higher. It wasn't as steady as he would have liked, but it was either go up or go back, so he went up.

One of the chinks of light was right above his head. He reached up with one hand and felt the old lumber that had fallen over the top of the shaft. Unlike the ladder, this was rotten. Roots dangled down, and bits of dirt fell on his head. He poked his hand carefully up through the hole and started making it larger. When it was big enough to put his head through, he climbed up another couple of steps and looked out.

He was, as he had suspected, on the rocky ridge just east of Thurston's house. He was only five or six feet higher than the driveway, a hundred yards away, and screened from observation by the oaks and hickories that grew there.

But he could see the house, at least its upper story. And he could hear people moving around outside.

He backed down a step, and carefully enlarged the hole so that he could get one arm up through it. Then he cleared away the leaves and twigs that covered the fallen shed wall, and as carefully as he could lifted one of the half-rotten boards aside. He had to turn his back to the house to climb out, and that made him nervous, but when he was free of the hole he turned and saw that he had been unobserved.

But he was exposed now. As long as he crouched down

low, the undergrowth—ferns, vines, hearts-a-bustin'—concealed him from casual observation. But if he stood, to better see what was going on next to the house and the nearer barn, he would be in full sight of anyone who might look that way.

He stayed low. Beyond the barns to the north was the fenced-in area he had spied on the night before. From his slightly elevated position, he could see the smaller enclosure with its low fence over which the Visitors had tossed the animals to bait out the crivit. It was too far away to make out any details, but he thought he recognized the machine that had winched in the crivit cage. Beyond the compound were the mounds of orange clay which had been dug out to make the sand-filled trench along which the crivit had come.

He brought his attention back to his present location. He made sure he knew exactly where the mine hole was and, crawling on hands and knees, skirted around the top of the shaft. It would not bear his weight if he should venture out onto the rotten boards that covered it. He moved through prickly weeds and greenbrier until he could see the driveway beside the house.

Two or three Visitors in red work uniforms were moving around just inside the door of the nearer barn, through which he could see only partway because of its angle to his line of sight. Once, one of them—a woman, he thought—came out carrying two animals, like groundhogs, but less chunky and with longer legs. Later, another Visitor came over to the near side of the barn and started a motor that ran a silage pump from the silo into the barn. After a while he came back and turned it off.

Durk tried to move to get a better view, but he was too exposed. If he put a tree between him and the barn door, he could be seen from the house. If he stood up, he could be seen from the entire farmyard. He'd had a half-formed idea of sneaking down to the house, maybe waylaying a Visitor or two, and then sneaking back, but there was too much activity going on, and he had no way to get any closer than he was without being seen.

Even as he watched, activity down in the yard between the house and the near barn became more intense. A kind of small cart with balloon tires was driven out of the far barn and over to the nearer one. Several Visitors came out of the barn, carrying cages in which two or three of the animals were held, and loaded them onto the flat bed of the car. When twelve of these cages had been loaded, one of the Visitors got into the seat at the front and drove it off into the compound and up along the side of the sand channel to the flats beyond the woods to the north.

Feeding time, he thought. He wished he knew what those smaller animals were. They were like nothing he'd ever seen before. The use of the silo to store their food told him that they were vegetarians, and that made sense. They would breed faster than the carnivores and would be used for their food. And the two that had been taken into the house were probably going to be eaten by the Visitors.

Beyond that, what he was seeing made little sense. He decided he'd taken enough of a risk, and keeping down, worked his way back to the mine shaft. He tried not to disturb the leaves too much, but he couldn't avoid leaving a bit of a track.

He got back to the hole, sat on the edge, and lowered himself down until his feet found a rung of the ladder. Then he turned once more, back to the house, just to make sure he hadn't been seen. If he had, nobody was doing anything about it. He climbed down the ladder to the bottom of the shaft, retrieved his flashlight, and started down the long tunnel to the river.

"I can't stand it anymore," Edna Knight cried while the other people in the barracks watched silently. "How can you people just sit here and take it?"

"Take it easy," Peter Frye said, trying to take her shoulders to make her sit down on her bunk. "You're not going to do anybody any good by yelling like that."

"So what should I do, let those guards paw me whenever they want?"

"That or let them beat you," Susan Green said.

"Well, I won't stand for it. I bet they don't fondle *your* precious body," she yelled at Peter and Dave Androvich, who had come up beside him.

"Don't bet on it," Dave said. "You watch those guards; they feel everybody up now and then."

"It's perverse," Edna insisted.

"It's worse than that," Chuck Lamont told her. "Maybe some of them do get a kick out of it, but they're really just checking to see how plump you are."

"Plump!" Edna was not exactly skinny. "What does plump have to do with it?"

"Why don't you just shut up," Peter told Chuck.

"Come on, Edna," Dave said, "let's go walk it off."

"No, wait a minute," Edna insisted, throwing off Dave's arm. "Come on, Chuck, what does being plump have to do with anything? They like their lovers fat?"

"Sorry," Chuck said, turning away, "I spoke out of turn."

"That guy who was squeezing my arm," Edna said, following him. "He was just making a pass, wasn't he?"

"Of course he was," Dave said. "They're all perverted."

"And you let them touch you?" Edna demanded, turning on Susan Green.

"What do you suggest as an alternative?" the older woman asked.

"Breaking out," Edna shouted. "My God, a child can climb over that fence. The guards all disappear at night. The woods aren't that far away. Come on, what are we waiting for, why does everybody let those damned lizards paw us and work us and violate our bodies and our minds?"

"Because we don't really have any choice," Bryan Ricardo said. He was just coming in from outside. "People can hear you halfway across the compound," he added.

"I don't care," Edna said, though she lowered her voice. "I've had enough. I'm getting out of here right now."

"Don't be stupid," Peter said. "You think they're going to let you just walk over the fence?"

"The worst they can do is shoot me," Edna said, starting toward the door. Peter reached out and grabbed her arm.

"You let go of me," she hissed, shaking herself free. She glared around at the people in the barracks. "You're such a bunch of sissies," she said, then stalked out.

"My God," Peter said, "why didn't anybody stop her?" He broke into a run and emerged from the barracks just in time to see Edna reach the chain-link fence.

Two guards, only fifty yards away, were watching with mild curiosity. Peter ran up to Edna as she started to climb.

"Don't be a fool," he shouted. Edna just lashed back with a foot, kicking him in the face and knocking him to the ground. The guards stood where they were and didn't even draw their sidearms.

"Edna," Peter called. "Come back." She ignored him, but other prisoners in the compound had heard the ruckus and had stopped to watch what was happening. Others came out of the various barracks buildings, and even a few more guards came to see.

"Nothing to it," Edna said from the top of the fence. She swung both legs over and dropped to the other side. Peter reached for the fence to try to follow her, but hands held him back.

"It's too late," Bryan said, dragging him away from the fence. Edna stood for a moment on the other side, just three feet away, looking back in. Her glance went to the guards nearby, who stood still, hands on their guns but with obviously no intention to draw.

"I don't believe it," Edna said. "We could have gotten out of here days ago." She turned and started across the broad sandy area that surrounded the compound.

She had gone not quite half the distance when something like a bubble in the sand, as big as a basketball, started moving toward her from off to one side.

"Oh, my God," Peter whispered as Edna, hearing the sussuration of the sand, turned to see what was making the sound. For a half second she just stood there, frozen. Then, with a small whimper breaking from her throat, she turned and started running back toward the fence.

The bubble in the sand hissed as it streaked toward her. She made three long strides before the wrist-thick tentacles reached up and grabbed her. She screeched once, and then the tentacles dragged her down under the sand, which roiled and tossed for a second or two. And then all was silent.

The guards, still calm, chuckled softly and turned away.

It was more difficult to climb up the riverbank from the tunnel's mouth than it had been to go down. The clay bank crumbled under Durk's hands and feet. But at last, red clay mingling on his clothes with the black dust of the tunnel, he managed to reach the top and pull himself up onto the thin strip of uncultivated land between the bank and his fields.

He brushed himself off as well as he could as he walked to his truck. Maybe, he thought, he ought to clean up a bit before going up to the Research Triangle Park. But the afternoon was wearing on, and he didn't want to take the chance of missing Dr. Van Oort, so he just drove on past his house and out onto the highway.

It took him twenty minutes to get to the bypass going around Chapel Hill, and from there another half hour to where Cornwallis crossed highway 54 in the RTP. The homeward-bound rush hour had already started.

He pulled into the parking lot in front of the futuristic-looking Diger-Fairwell building. There were few cars left. He walked into the front lobby and up to the reception desk. There was only one woman on duty. She looked up as he neared.

"My name is Durk Attweiler," he said. "I'd like to see Dr. Van Oort, if she's still here."

The receptionist looked at him and though she was trained to be polite, it was obvious that she doubted if he had any legitimate business here. Durk felt self-conscious in this center of high research and was painfully aware of the state of his clothes. He forced himself to stand still and not brush at the mud and dust.

The receptionist picked up a phone and dialed a number, rather than letting him do it himself. "Dr. Van Oort," she said, "there's a man named Attweiler here to see you." The response must have surprised her. "Yes, Doctor, I'll have somebody show him up."

She hung up, obviously curious that someone as important and busy as the research director would find time to see a dirty farmer. "Louie?" she called to a security guard who was standing at the far side of the huge lobby. "Will you take Mr. Attweiler up to Dr. Van Oort's office, please?"

The guard came over to the desk, and the receptionist filled out and handed Durk a visitor's sticker, which he stuck onto his shirt pocket.

"This way, please," the guard said, and led him up stairs, down a hall, through a secretarial foyer, then down another hall to a large office.

The woman behind the desk surprised him. From his conversations with Arnold Rutgers and JoAnn Hirakawa the other day, he had expected Dr. Van Oort to be a vigorous foreign-looking gentleman instead of a small older woman.

"Mr. Attweiler," Dr. Van Oort said as he paused hesitantly in the doorway. "Please come in." He did so and the security guard left. "In here," she said, gesturing toward the bug-free parlor adjacent to her office. "Sit down, please," she invited with a smile as she followed him in.

"I'll get your chair dirty," Durk said apologetically.

"Doesn't matter. At least it will be good Carolina clay, and not green alien blood. Rutgers and Corey were a mess."

"How's Wendel?" Durk asked, sitting gingerly.

"He's going to be just fine. Nothing broken, just a few sprains. You probably saved his life by acting as quickly as you did."

"Didn't have time to think about it," Durk said.

"It was courageous anyway. And we appreciate your help in getting one of those monsters."

"You can have all you want. Uh, look, I don't know if you're the right person to talk to, but somebody ought to know." He told her about the mine tunnel leading to the ridge beside the Visitors' house, and what he'd seen there.

"Yes," Dr. Van Oort said when he'd finished. "That could be very important. We knew they were keeping a smaller species of herbivore, but didn't know what for. As for the mine, I'll tell the people who can make the best use of that information."

"I figure," Durk said slowly, "that about six guys could take the lizards out if they snuck in that way at night."

"I'm sure they could, Mr. Attweiler, and I know you're not happy with the Visitors breeding monsters like those crivits that close to your farm. But before we do anything drastic, we want to learn all we can about what they're doing and why."

"They're breeding monsters," Durk said tightly.

"That's true, but to what purpose? Just to make better prison camp guards? Then why not do that at the camps? We suspect that the Visitors intend to set these monsters loose in certain places, which will make those places very unsafe for humans. Do crivits eat Visitors? If they do, then those places would be unsafe for them too, but if they don't eat Visitors, then they could use those areas while we would be kept out of them. Unless, of course, there's some more complex reason. And that's why we won't shut down their laboratory until we know more. And, if we can, until we know how to detect crivits underground and learn how to deal with them effectively."

"Yeah," Durk said unenthusiastically. "I see what you're talking about. It's just that it's *my* fields those things are running around in."

"I'm sorry, Mr. Attweiler."

"That's all right." He got to his feet. "But if you ever want to use that mine, just let me know."

"We will," Dr. Van Oort said, getting up to shake his

hand. "And we'll appreciate anything further you might learn about your neighbors and their pets." She led him to the outer office. Louie, the guard, was waiting outside the door to take Durk back to the lobby.

After Durk left, Lucia Van Oort closed up her office and walked to the other end of the building where the surgical laboratories were. Bringing the crivit in without being stopped at a checkpoint had been something of a trick, but they'd managed it, and now the monster was in lab B, where Penny Carmichal, JoAnn Hirakawa, and Arnold Rutgers were already at work when Lucia arrived.

It was not a large lab and was normally used for smaller animals like rabbits, but it was accessed only through lab A, and the door could be concealed if Visitors ever took it into their minds to come through on an inspection tour. Diger-Fairwell had no deep basements as Data Tronix did, and Lucia just hoped that this makeshift security was adequate.

Her three subordinates did no more than glance up when she entered. The crivit was stretched out on two metal tables set end to end, but even so the tentacles around its mouth dangled, the two longest ones reaching the floor. Over the creature, cameras mounted on ceiling tracks were sliding back and forth, changing angle, aperture, and magnification as Penny keyed in commands at the control console.

"We're using up a lot of videotape," Arnold said as Lucia came over to stand beside him. "The thing is changing colors and its tentacles are shrinking."

"It smells," Lucia said.

"It does," JoAnn agreed, "and it's getting worse. It's not like anything I've ever smelled before either."

"I wish you could have taken it alive," Lucia said.

"So do we," Arnold told her, "but we'd have needed twice as many men and a bigger winch, and then I don't know how we'd have gotten it into a cage."

"The Visitors have a method," Lucia said, "according to Mr. Attweiler."

"You think the Visitors would let us build a special trap

up on the sand flats?" JoAnn asked. "We'd have to do like they did—dig the trap first and then connect it with a trench."

"I know," Lucia said, unruffled. "Just wishful thinking."

Penny finished with her pictures, so they turned the monster over onto its back. "We shot this side first," Penny explained. "That was just the way it went onto the table."

JoAnn took a pair of surgical gloves and started drawing them on. "Ready to open it up?" she asked.

"That's what I'm here for," Arnold said.

As he worked, with JoAnn assisting, Penny took more pictures of each step. He slit the skin, peeled it back, checking the underlying musculature, locating the thoracic and abdominal cavities. The latter he opened up at once, to remove the stomach and bowels and their contents, to keep them from accelerating the creature's decay.

"It's a female," he said as he carefully lifted organs aside and removed them to be placed in preservative for later study. He reached in and gently removed a long tube of flesh, in which could be seen half a dozen bulges. He lay this down on the exposed rib cage and slit it open. Inside were six white, spherical eggs, each the size of a softball.

"Let's get those into an incubator," Lucia suggested. "Just in case one hatches." Since the others were busy, she went herself back into lab A to retrieve the desired equipment. When she brought it back, JoAnn carefully put the eggs into it.

"We took the crivit's temperature," she said, "as soon as we got it in, and given the amount of time it had been dead, I think I can make a good guess as to its internal temperature when it was alive." She set the controls on the portable incubator, which Lucia then took back to lab A. Gordon Lloyd, a technician who had been taken into their confidence, came in as she was pushing the incubator into its place against the wall.

"We just got a phone call from Data Tronix," he said.

"Tell me about it in here," Lucia told him, and led him into lab B.

For a long moment, Gordon could say nothing at all, but just looked at the monster on the tables.

"She-it," he said at last. "Goddamn." He shook his head and swallowed a couple of times, hard. "That's what the phone call was about," he said, nodding at the monster. "Dr. Marino said they had made some progress on the 'silicon project.' That's the 'silicon project,' huh?"

"Makes you want to stay away from the beaches, doesn't it?" Penny said.

"That isn't funny," Gordon told her. "Dr. Marino also said her 'friends' were going to 'start a production' at 'The Dunes.'" He turned to Lucia. "She wants you and Arnold to come over."

"I can't," Arnold said. "Gordon, you've been drafted as my assistant. JoAnn, you go with Dr. Van Oort."

"Right," JoAnn said, peeling off her gloves. "You'll get used to it after a while," she told Gordon as he reluctantly went to get a fresh pair of gloves for himself.

Without wasting any further time, Lucia and JoAnn left.

Anne Marino met Lucia and JoAnn in the lobby and took them down to the secret lab below Data Tronix where Mark Casey, Steve Wong, and Shirley Patchek were already waiting. "We've gotten some interesting messages," Anne explained, "and we thought we'd better let you in on them so you can tell us whether we ought to be concerned about the implications."

"You think the Visitors are going to let crivits loose down at the beaches?"

"Something like that," Mark said. "Apparently Leon had made some kind of report to Diana, which we couldn't tap, of course, not having a bug at the breeding station, but if we read it correctly, Diana called Chang shortly after that and had her call Leon. At first, except for mentioning Leon, we didn't know that Diana's conversation with Chang had anything to do with crivits. You know how it goes: when you both know what you're talking about, you don't bother recapitulating like they do in bad fiction—'As you know, Chang, those crivits guard our prison camps' and so on. But then when Diana hung up, Chang immediately called Leon and warned him about following through with his plans without Diana's approval.''

''And those plans,'' Anne said, ''appear to include taking breeding pairs of this new variety of crivit to certain locations we haven't been able to identify, and there let them go.''

''I keep on feeling,'' Steve Wong said, ''that there's more to it than that, but I can't point to any particular phrase or sentence in the transcriptions to support that.''

''That could be pretty disruptive all by itself,'' JoAnn said. ''You know what the crivits have done over at Attweiler's farm.''

''We know they're chewing up one of his fields,'' Steve said, ''and that you had a hell of a time catching one this afternoon.''

''Crivits are pretty nasty,'' JoAnn said, and described the one they'd caught to the computer scientists.

''My God,'' Anne said, ''we can't have creatures like that running loose all up and down the East Coast.''

''That would take care of tourism on the beaches, for sure,'' Steve agreed.

''It may not be as bad as we think,'' Lucia said. ''Crivits are strongly limited in two ways. First, they can't go where the soil is too dense. Attweiler's field is just marginal. Put one out in your front yard, and it would be helpless. And second, as a carnivore it needs a large prey population. Though we think it's reptile, it eats the way a mammal does—as do the Visitors too, of course. The sandy areas of the East Coast tend to have less wildlife than elsewhere, and so the number of crivits can't ever get too large.''

''You don't need many tigers,'' Steve said, ''to make the jungle dangerous.''

''I agree,'' Lucia replied, ''and that's the real threat. Not that crivits will multiply extravagantly, but that even one is enough to make a farm unusable, a beach too hazardous to visit. It isn't that people will be eaten in large numbers, but that thousands of acres of land will be unavailable to us, and some of that land is valuable for reasons other than tourism or crops. Imagine what would happen down at Fort Bragg, for example, with all the sand they've got there."

"Rather academic," Mark said, "since the base has been closed."

"True, but there are other places. No, I agree, the monsters have to be stopped, but for economic reasons rather than because they're a great threat to human life."

"The trick is," JoAnn said, "that once they're loose, you have no idea where they are. Where their environment is marginal, you can hear them burrowing, but the softer the sand, the more quiet they are."

"So what are we going to do about it?" Mark asked. "If Leon doesn't have Diana's full approval, we might stop him by letting Diana know what he's up to and letting her take care of it."

"We don't know that she would," Anne said, "and besides, if we lodged any kind of complaint, they'd know that their headquarters were bugged, and we'd lose whatever advantage we have because of that."

"But if we don't," Steve said, "we may lose control of a large portion of the East Coast. What good are bugs then?"

"We need to know more," Lucia said. "Obviously, part of the problem is that you don't have any direct intelligence from the breeding station. If you could get a bug on their lines, that could make a lot of difference."

"We could give it a try," Steve said dubiously, "if we can just get ourselves *to* the place without being seen."

"That may be possible," Lucia said, and told them about the mine Durk Attweiler had described to her.

"That sounds interesting," Mark said. "We'll have to check that out."

"Especially," Shirley said, "if that will give us a clue as to where this Camp T-3 is."

"I don't know about that," Lucia said.

The computer scientists filled her in on what they'd been able to learn of the secret prison camp so far. "If we can locate the place," Mark concluded, "we might be able to help a few people escape. Would Corey and Fenister be interested in a project like that?"

"I'm sure they would," JoAnn said, "but Fenister isn't going to be doing much for the next few days." She explained about his minor but disabling injuries.

"I don't think we're ready for that kind of rebel activity," Lucia said. "We've been lucky that there's been practically no fighting in the Triangle area, but at the same time that means we have nobody who's had combat experience."

"I know," Mark said, "but we're going to have to start sometime."

Leon and Freda walked between the stacks of verlog cages. The animals inside seemed to be doing well—they were healthy and plump.

"The breeding rate for this variety," Freda said, "is very good. Four litters a year, ten pups each, and they reach breeding maturity in half a year."

"They're also tastier than the more common variety," Leon said. "Of course, it takes a lot of food to keep them going, but we should have no trouble with that."

"They'll taste even better," Freda said, "when they have access to natural forage instead of this silage." She led him over to a series of cages kept separate from the others, against the side wall of the barn toward the back. "Like these," she said. "This group has been getting mostly oak and hickory." Instead of feed troughs, these cages had a special box on the front into which leaves and twigs had been stuffed. "These here have been fed pine—it gives an interesting piquancy to the taste. Cedar makes the flesh a bit too strong. Sweetgum, though, and yellow poplar are also nice."

"Let's have one along with dinner tonight," Leon suggested, "as a treat."

"Sounds good to me," Freda said. She reached into one

of the cages where a verlog slightly smaller than a cat was munching on yellow-poplar leaves. The animal froze as her hand touched it. She lifted it out, closed the cage, and the other animals inside went back to their perpetual eating.

"Ever tried human?" Freda asked as they took the animal out of the barn.

"Once. Very complex flavor, as you'd guess from their mixed diet. How about you?"

"One time. Too sweet for my taste."

They went into the "kitchen" of the house and handed the verlog to Edmond, whose turn it was to prepare supper that night. He already had the serving cages of birds and rodents set out, so he started to prepare the verlog at once while Freda went to call the others. He was an expert butcher and had the cups of blood and plates of meat strips all ready by the time the rest of the staff had assembled.

They had just started eating when the communicator in the upstairs office chimed.

"Damn," Leon said. He picked up one slice of verlog and went up to answer the call.

He chewed the meat, instead of just swallowing it whole, in order to savor the subtle spiciness of the flavor. He sat at the communicator, hit the "acknowledge" button, and gulped hurriedly when Diana's image came on the screen.

"I'm sorry to interrupt your supper," Diana said, not sounding sorry at all. "I assume Administrator Chang gave you my message earlier today."

"Yes, Diana, she did. I was disappointed to receive it, but I agree that your objections are valid."

"We cannot risk destroying this environment," Diana said, "the way we did our own back home. Your ideas are bold, Leon, but I'm not sure you fully appreciate the consequences."

"I think I do," Leon said, "now that you have brought them to my attention." There was only the faintest trace of sarcasm in his voice.

"Very well then. What have you done about your security?"

"We will install the sand fence tomorrow. That, of course, is not critical. As for the verlogs, all have been brought indoors. Of course, that makes things a little crowded."

"Be that as it may, Leon, I'll feed you to the crivits myself if you let this project of yours get out of hand. Our past relationships notwithstanding."

"I understand, Diana."

The screen went blank. He turned off the communicator, sighed, and got to his feet. The taste of fresh verlog was still in his mouth. There wouldn't be any left for him by the time he got back downstairs, of course.

Chapter 8

When Durk heard the sound of a car coming up his drive, he put away his homemade whiskey and rinsed his mouth before going out onto the porch to see who it was. It was getting dark, but he recognized Arnold Rutgers as he got out from the driver's seat. The other three were strangers to him.

"Good evening," Arnold called. "I hope we're not disturbing you."

"Not at all," Durk said. "Come on in the house." He stepped back to let Arnold and the three others, one of them a woman, into his living room.

"We'd like to take a look at that tunnel you told Dr. Van Oort about," Arnold said after he'd introduced Mark Casey, Anne Marino, and Steve Wong. "If it's not too late."

"Shouldn't make any difference," Durk said. "Tunnels don't care if it's day or night outside. What do you have in mind?"

"Two things," Mark said. "First, just to get an idea of the layout of the Visitors' place, in case we decide we have to do anything about them being there. But perhaps more important, to see whether we can bug their communications system so that we can find out what they're up to."

"Aside from breeding monsters, you mean. Well, they're breeding some kind of other animal too, as I told Dr. Van Oort. As to what they're going to do with them, I can't tell you."

"That's one of the things we want to find out," Anne said.

"You planning on going with us?" Durk asked.

"I helped bug their headquarters building up in the Research Triangle Park," Anne told him.

"Then I guess you're qualified. Be best to wait a bit, though, till it gets full dark. I don't think those lizards are watching my place, but it doesn't pay to take any chances."

"You're a very cautious man," Steve said.

"It pays to be," Durk said shortly, looking meaningfully at Arnold.

"I think these folks might be a little better off for a sample of your handiwork," Arnold said.

"Not much of it left," Durk said. "Got to brew up another batch—when I get the chance." He went to get his last bottle of moonshine and some glasses. "Just one for the road," he said when he came back to the living room. "Keep the chill off." He handed out glasses and poured each one just a tot. Mark and Steve looked at their glasses uncertainly, but Anne sniffed the whiskey once, then tossed it off.

"You do good work," she said as Arnold followed suit.

"Thank you, ma'am. We'll have another when we get back." He watched as Mark and Steve tentatively sipped their moonshine. "It's not white lightning," he said. "That's just made with sugar and water. This is made from corn. Of course, it hasn't been aged much," he added critically.

"Not bad," Mark said, almost sounding as if he believed it. Steve didn't say anything and didn't finish his drink either.

"We'll leave the lights on when we go," Durk said. "And I think we'd better walk. You got anything you want to bring along?"

"It's in the car," Mark said.

"Then maybe we should be going. It's kind of the long way round, and you'll want to be able to see something when we get there."

He got his big flashlight, and they left the house. The others waited while Mark went to the car and came back with an attaché case. Then, keeping his house between them and the Thurston place, Durk led them across the fields toward the river.

At the bank he turned them north and they went up through the low undergrowth under the occasional trees. "Watch your step going down," he cautioned as he started down the bank. He went slowly so that the others would be able to follow in the growing dark.

When they were all safely in the mine tunnel, he turned on his light and led them toward the mine head. "Can't get lost," he said as they passed an occasional side tunnel, "if you just keep going straight. No turns at all between the river and the ladder."

They had to go up the ladder one at a time, since it wasn't strong enough to bear two of them at once. Durk went first, to make sure the coast was clear, and as each of the others got to the surface, he made them lie down among the weeds and vines.

There were plenty of lights on at the Visitors' house, but the driveway and yard were dark. No lights burned in either of the two barns.

"The near barn," Durk said softly, "is where the other animals are kept. The barn in back is their garage and machine shop, I think."

"Let's go down and take a look," Anne said. She got to her feet—crawling would take too long, be too noisy, and would leave her too vulnerable should she have to flee—and started down the gentle slope. Mark and Steve immediately followed suit. Durk hesitated a moment, finding it a bit difficult to digest the fact of Anne's leadership. He remembered his condescending question back at the house and felt acute embarrassment. Then he too, with Arnold beside him, started down toward the barn.

They kept the barn between them and the house the whole way, but the door to the barn was within plain sight of the house and whoever might be looking out. Whispering to the others to stay where they were, Anne slid along the front of the barn to the door and tried the latch. Apparently it wasn't locked, since she slid the door open at once, just far enough for her to slip inside. As she did so, the other four quickly followed. When they were all in, Anne slid the door shut again but left a finger-wide crack through which they could watch for sudden arrivals.

Durk heard a small clicking, like a latch being undone, and then saw Mark holding a flashlight which had been carefully taped so that only a dim glow emanated from its lens. Mark snapped the attaché case back shut, and they looked around at the rows of cages stacked to the ceiling.

"What are they?" Steve asked.

"I don't know," Durk said, "but they feed them to the crivits, and they eat them themselves, I think." There was very little animal smell in the place, and Durk found that most disturbing.

"They're vegetarians," Arnold said, going from cage to cage. "Mammals, obviously. Their feet look like they're good at climbing. They're being bred, see? All the cages have two adults, but those with infants have been divided to keep the male away from the litter."

"I'd guess," Mark said as he and the others followed along behind Arnold, "that this animal was the Visitors' main food supply on their ships."

"Quite possible. I can't tell from such a hurried look, but I think they probably breed rather quickly and reach maturity quickly. And can eat almost any vegetable matter."

"This is all very interesting," Anne said, "but we'd better get those bugs on their communications lines."

They made their way back to the door where Anne stood a moment, peering through the crack. Then she put her ear up to it and listened.

"We're clear," she said as Mark turned off the light. Anne opened the door and as Steve went through, whispered something to him. He nodded and, moving quickly in a low crouch, went to the wall of the house and pressed himself against it, between two windows. Mark followed and did the same, as did Arnold and Durk. Anne, the last one out, paused only to slide the barn door shut before joining the others.

They were fortunate in that both the power and the phone lines were connected at this side of the house. Mark opened his case again, relying on the light of the windows without actually moving into it, and handed Steve several items.

"Keep an eye on the front of the house," Anne whispered to Durk. "I'll watch toward the back."

"Somebody ought to look into that other barn," Mark murmured.

"I'll do it," Arnold said, and moved off in that direction.

Durk went toward the front corner of the house. Kneeling low to the ground, he peered around it until he could see the front porch. There was nobody there. He looked back over his shoulder and saw Mark at the phone connection, fiddling with something, while Steve worked at the power lines. He turned away, and instead of watching, unfocused his eyes and concentrated on listening to the night.

He could just barely hear subtle bumps and hums, footsteps and conversation, coming from somewhere in the house. That was as it should be. Once or twice there were other sounds, mechanical or electrical, which he couldn't identify. That was okay too. He could also hear an occasional snip or tap from where Mark and Steve were working. Unless they struck the walls of the house, the Visitors inside should not notice.

A "pssst" coming from behind him brought him around sharply.

"We've got company," he heard Mark whisper. He saw Anne and Arnold coming from the back of the house, moving quickly and low, near the wall. Durk left his post and went to join them.

"What is it?" Durk asked.

"Somebody coming back from that compound you saw the other night," Arnold said. "Wasn't it at about this time that you saw them feeding the crivits?"

"Damn poor timing," Mark muttered. "At least I got the tap in."

"Me too," Steve said, "but I may not have it hooked up right."

"Can't worry about that now," Anne said. "Let's get out of here." One by one, swiftly and as quietly as they could, they moved to the north side of the barn, past a kerosene tank up on stanchions, and to the far side away from the house.

All except Arnold, who moved instead to the door and went inside.

"What the hell's he doing?" Mark whispered angrily. Durk could hear two Visitors talking casually to each other as they approached from the crivit compound.

"Probably getting a sample," Anne said. The two crivit feeders neared, and Durk, flat on his stomach to look around the corner of the barn, saw them coming from behind the garage and shop building. The door of the barn started to slide open but moved less than an inch before it stopped. The two Visitors went up to the back door of the porch, and without entering talked to someone inside. Arnold took that moment when their eyes were adjusted to brighter light and their attention directed to whomever was inside to slip out of the barn and close the door behind him. He did not run, for fear of making noise or falling, but slid quickly along the front of the barn to the corner. Durk got to his feet as the veterinary surgeon came around.

"Damn fool," Mark hissed.

"Got 'em," Arnold whispered triumphantly, holding two of the small animals.

"Let's go!" Anne whispered. Durk took the lead and they followed him away from the barn toward the slope and the woods. Again, they did not run, deeming it more important to be silent than swift. Behind them, they could hear the Visitors' heavy footfalls as they approached the barn, the grate as the door slid open, and a moment later light beamed from the back windows.

One of the beams shone squarely upon them. Someone

on the back porch of the house, from which they were no longer concealed, shouted.

"That's it," Mark said. "Let's move."

Durk ran up the slope toward the mine head. Behind him he could hear his companions following and behind them the Visitors in pursuit. He stopped suddenly when he realized that he'd lost the top of the mine shaft.

"Be carerful," he told the others. "If you step on it, you'll fall through."

"But they're coming," Steve said, and indeed they were—not running but moving with purposefulness, aided by strong flashlights. Durk looked back at the house, then the barn, then moved toward the oncoming Visitors and a bit to the right. When his perspective of house and barn were correct, he went to his knees.

"Here," he called softly. The others came even as the first beams of the flashlights played around them. Durk helped Steve into the hole, then Mark, Arnold next, and last Anne. When he slipped in himself the whole area was illuminated, and shouts from the Visitors told him he'd been seen.

The ladder creaked under their weight but did not break. Durk dropped the last few feet, grabbed the bottom of the ladder, and jerked it away so that it half fell, half slid into the main tunnel.

"That will hold them for a little bit," he said even as strong lights speared down from the top of the shaft. An alien handgun snapped, and a bolt of energy struck the floor by his foot, leaving the stone glowing red.

"They won't be held up for long," Arnold said as they hurried down the tunnel.

And it wasn't long enough. Whether the Visitors jumped or had some kind of ladder with them, they never knew, but they'd gone only a few hundred feet when light speared down the tunnel after them, followed by more shots.

There was no choice but to duck into one of the side tunnels. Durk paused at the junction, and when the first Visitor, Gerald, came around, smashed him in the face.

Gerald staggered back, his eyes wide, recognizing Durk even in his shock. Durk kicked him hard in the groin and then ran to join his friends.

He would have missed them if Mark hadn't turned on his flash for a moment to look into another side branch. At first they mistook him for a Visitor, and he barely avoided being struck down himself. They could hear the other Visitors behind them, and reflected light beams bounced off the walls.

"This way," Durk said. He thought he recognized his location by the tools left lying on the ground, but when they came to the next intersection, he was completely lost.

"Where are we?" Anne asked.

"I don't know," Durk said.

"Turn off the flash," Arnold suggested, and Mark did so. They were plunged into complete darkness. "Now listen," Arnold added, and fell silent. They listened. Somewhere far away they could hear Visitor voices calling back and forth.

They waited. After a while the voices faded away.

"Now," Arnold said, "I think it will be safe to try to find our way back."

They used the standard maze-following procedure of always turning in the same direction. Durk knew that the mines were not all that extensive, compared to those that had produced more gold, but there were more tunnels, intersections, and galleries than he had been aware of.

Mark used the flash only when necessary. Durk did not use his at all, in case they should need it later. Instead, they walked by feel, keeping their hands on the side wall, and sliding their feet forward to check for potholes and shafts. Only when they came to an intersection did they turn on the light briefly, in the hopes of finding themselves in a familiar place. They never did.

After about two hours Steve, who was taking the lead, saw a gray light coming up a side tunnel. They went to it, hoping it was the main tunnel to the riverbank, but when they got to it they found themselves instead in a place where the roof of the tunnel had collapsed. The light, brighter here, was only the reflected moonlight, which now shone down into the hole.

The cave-in had left rocks and dirt piled up high enough so that they were able, with some difficulty, to crawl up out of the ground. They now stood on the side of a thinly forested hill. Off one way they could see the headlights of a car perhaps a quarter mile away as it went down a road.

"Any ideas?" Anne asked.

"I think so," Durk said. He looked up at the moon. "What time is it?" Mark told him. "That would mean that's U.S. Fifty-six," Durk said, pointing to where they'd seen the car's headlights. "That way's east. We've come up on the north side."

"Can you get us back to your place from here?" Steve asked.

"It may take awhile," Durk said, "but at least we can't get lost."

"Then let's get going," Arnold said, shifting the animals in his arms. "These are getting heavy."

Morton Barnes had just settled down to rehearse his notes for his 9 A.M. class when the door of his office opened and three armed Visitors marched in.

"Professor Barnes," the one in the middle said, "will you come with us, please." It was not a question.

He was quickly taken downstairs to an all-white Visitor paddywagon waiting in the parking lot. His guards did not talk with him as they drove through Chapel Hill toward the Eastgate shopping center. They did not talk to him as they took him from the paddywagon and led him into a skyfighter standing in the parking lot. He was put into a tiny cabin alone.

The flight did not take very long, but it gave him plenty of time to think, to feel sick, to wonder whether his arrest was because of his conversation with Jozef or because of something else he had said or done. His anxiety and his confusion made his head spin, and he was almost glad when the skyfighter landed and he could stop thinking.

He was taken from the skyfighter and down from the roof of a building into a large room where he was searched, questioned, and passed on. He left the building by another door and found himself in a compound, with barrackslike buildings along the sides, surrounded by a chain-link fence. Other people were standing around, their clothes rumpled, the men with growths of beard.

"Professor Barnes," someone said, and he looked around to see Dave Androvich and several other people walking toward him. "Welcome to Camp T-3." Dave's tone was eminently sardonic. "What did you do to deserve this honor?"

"I don't know, Dave. They haven't told me anything."

"And they won't either," a short, well-muscled, and very angry young man of Dave's age said. "We know why *we're* here, but only because they caught us red-handed."

"This is Peter Frye," Dave said. "We tried to sabotage the lizards' headquarters on campus."

"I heard about that," Barnes said. "Weren't there some others?"

"Greta Saroyan," Peter said. "She's in there." He nodded at a building in a secondary compound. "Edna Knight—she's dead. Tried to run across the sand moat that surrounds the place. And Benny Mounds. They took him and Susan Green away last night." His voice was beginning to get frantic. "Apparently Benny and Susan did well on their tests. They're going to be converted."

"Oh, my God," Barnes said. He looked with shock at the other two men with Dave and Greta.

"Sorry, Professor," Dave said. "This is Cliff Upton and Bryan Ricardo. They've been helping us get used to this place."

Barnes did little more than nod in greeting. "At least," he said, "they haven't taken *you* off for conversion yet."

"That's just the point," Peter said, almost shouting. "Nobody knows for sure, but if you ask around, you can figure it out. Either you're useful and they convert you, or you're not—like us."

"Peter hasn't gotten used to the idea," Cliff Upton said. "I don't like it much myself, but it's that or try to make it across the crivit patch."

"I don't understand," Barnes said.

"The crivit patch," Upton started to explain. "That's that sandy area just outside the fence—"

"I don't mean that," Barnes interrupted. "What do they do to you if they don't convert you—make you slave labor?"

"For a while," Peter said, "until you're fat enough."

"And then they eat you," Bryan finished.

In spite of her exertions of the night before and only a few hours' sleep since, Anne Marino still had a division to supervise. She sat in her office now, trying to stay awake as she examined reports of work in progress. Data Tronix, in spite of the alien occupation, still did a lot of business, and it was up to Anne to see that part of it was done well, efficiently, and on time.

Her intercom buzzed. "Mark, here," the voice at the other end said. He sounded as tired as she felt. "Our silicon analysts are here. Can I bring them up?"

"Sure," she said, though it took her a moment to realize what he was talking about. She put her papers away and started making coffee in the machine in the corner of her office. The pot was half full when Mark came in with Penny Carmichal and JoAnn Hirakawa.

"I think we're going to have to destroy the crivit ranch right away," JoAnn said without preamble.

"But we've just installed the bugs," Anne protested.

"I know," Penny said, "and I think we'll have a few days before things start to get critical, but we've been comparing old reports, examining the adult that was brought in, and watching the eggs from it."

"They survived," JoAnn said, "and hatched. We've had

them long enough now to run a few simple tests. And even with infants, what we've learned is frightening."

"Young crivits," Penny said as Mark went to pour the coffee, "can eat up to their full body weight within two hours of catching their prey. Within a day they increase their size by twenty-five percent. They won't eat for a while after that—just how long we're not sure. If they're starved, they just lie in wait and lose very little weight in the process."

"The frightening part is," JoAnn said, "that they are sexually mature on hatching, or at least appear to be. The adult had a reservoir of semen in her body, and my guess is that on maturity, they start to develop eggs after each feeding, instead of continuing to increase in size."

"The net result is," Penny went on, "that one mature female crivit can produce ten offspring after each feeding. Offspring reach egg-laying age in what we estimate to be about three months, if they have sufficient food to grow continually during that time. Nine of the ten eggs we hatched were female, and incest doesn't seem to bother them. So at the end of three months you now have ten breeding females instead of one, and after six months you have a hundred."

"Given a sufficient quantity of food," JoAnn said. "And God knows, those crivits eat anything they can drag down. Snails, insects, rodents, earthworms."

"There's still a predator-prey ratio to be preserved," Penny said. "We estimate that prey mass must be at least one hundred to two hundred times the mass of the crivit population. That's not so bad, but in most environments, there are a number of predator species in competition, some prey is considered unsuitable, and natural prey has evolved strategies in their favor. With crivits, none of these apply."

"You mean they could destroy all life on the East Coast?" Anne asked at last.

"No, not at all," JoAnn said. "Things would stabilize in a decade or so when the crivit population expanded to its feeding capacity. We would have just as much wildlife as before. But it would be a different balance. Imagine what life would be like if wolf packs, lion prides, and families of bears roamed around without our ability to kill them off. The ecological system would shift radically. It would survive, though a number of species might die out from overpreying or inadequate competition with the crivits. But human economics would go down the tubes."

"And since," Mark interjected, "some of these crivits have already gotten beyond the confines of the breeding station, we'll have to stop them before they escape altogether."

"I won't argue with you," Anne said, "but this is going to have to be carefully planned. We'll have to take out Leon and his staff all at once. Then we'll have to make sure we catch and kill all the crivits. And we'll have to do that quickly, before Chang finds out something is wrong and comes down to stop us. If we miss on this one shot, we won't have a second chance."

"I agree," Mark said. "But we might be able to accomplish our ends in another way. Remember that conversation Diana had with Leon the other day? She warned him against allowing that very thing to happen, letting the crivits escape. Maybe it's time we admitted we've bugged the place, and sent word to Chang that Leon is endangering the environment and working against Diana's explicit instructions."

"I think we may be able to blow the whistle on Leon," Anne said, "without having to divulge our own big secret. All we have to do is admit that we've bugged the breeding lab, which we have."

"We'll work all three ways," Mark said. "Personally, I think we could do a lot just by killing Leon. He's the one, after all, who's responsible. If he were out of the picture, I don't think anybody else would be allowed to carry on in his stead."

"It's obvious," JoAnn said, "that we've got a lot more thinking to do, and I—"

"Just a minute," Anne said as the intercom buzzed.

"This is Bill," said the voice on the other end. "Use the green line, please."

Anne picked up the phone and punched the button that opened the dedicated line not connected to the outside world. Whether the Visitors had taps on their other phone lines was uncertain, but this line was isolated and inspected daily.

"What is it, Bill?" she asked.

"Professor Morton Barnes was arrested this morning and taken to Camp T-3."

"Damn," Anne said. "Thanks, Bill." She hung up and told the others the news.

"Damn, indeed," JoAnn said. "Barnes knows all about us. If they question him, they'll be sure to find out, and then everything will be over."

"I guess this puts the crivits on hold," Mark said.

"Only as far as a decision is concerned," Anne told him and the others. "I want everybody to come up with every possible plan they can, and we'll talk about it later. But you're right, if we don't get Barnes out of Camp T-3, none of our plans will have any meaning."

A short while later, Anne drove through downtown Chapel Hill toward Carrboro. Traffic seemed normal, and there were few Visitors in sight. She drove up Greensboro Street in Carrboro to the FCX, where she parked and went inside.

Wilma Southerland and another woman were attending to customers at the counter. Anne waited until Wilma was free, and then went up to her.

"There's something about my last bill I don't understand," she said. "Can I talk to you about it?"

"Surely," Wilma said. "Come on into the office." She lifted the flap on the counter and led Anne into the back room.

"We need some professional help," Anne said when Wilma had shut the door.

"What sort?" Wilma asked, lighting a cigarette.

"The lizards picked up someone who knows enough about us to endanger the whole intelligence project," Anne said, and told about Professor Barnes's arrest and what he knew.

"That's bad," Wilma agreed. "Underground central has been able to put a lot of your information to good use. Not to mention that your own lives will be in danger."

"There's a complication," Anne said, and told her the most recent developments in the crivit project. "We just don't have the personnel or the expertise to handle both situations at once," she concluded. "I'm not even sure we can make the right decision ourselves."

"Boy, you've really opened up a can of worms," Wilma said. "All right, this calls for the best. I'll get a message to Chris Faber out in L.A. and call you back on it as soon as I know anything."

"Thanks, Wilma," Anne said. They left the office. "Thanks for clearing that up for me," she added as Wilma let her out from behind the counter.

"No problem," Wilma said, and turned to take care of the next customer.

RTP Area Administrator Chang looked over the report she had just received from the crivit research project. A brief message telling of the human trespass had been waiting for her when she'd gotten to her office a few hours ago. It also said a full report would be forthcoming. As she read it now, she tried to convince herself that it was just a case of random vandalism, as had happened on the UNC Chapel Hill campus awhile back.

According to the report, there had been no damage, but two verlogs had turned up missing. Whether these had been taken by the humans or whether the humans had just allowed them to escape, nobody knew. Their disappearance might not have had anything to do with the trespass, since the staff occasionally supplemented their meals with one of the test animals.

Of greater interest was the discovery, during pursuit of

the humans, of the mines underneath the Thurston property. The full extent of the mine tunnels had not yet been determined, but their existence seemed to provide no hazard to the house or the other buildings on the property. That the humans had used the mines to gain access to the property was worrisome, however. Besides the mind head just a few hundred yards from the house, there were three other exits, and the humans could have entered from any one of these.

Chang read the descriptions of the five humans involved. None were very clear, but one rang a bell. It was a more complete description than the others, since the man had been seen up close by Gerald, one of the technicians on the crivit project. And though Visitors found that most humans seemed to look alike, Chang felt sure that she had seen this same person herself once or twice before.

She reached for the communicator and called Leon at the crivit farm.

"I've just finished reading your report," she said when Leon came on the line. "This human who Gerald saw— does his description seem at all familiar to you?"

"It does," Leon said, "but I haven't been able to place it."

"That narrows it down quite a bit," Chang said. "The only place we've been together where there are humans is the Five Star Bar."

"That's it," Leon said. "He was sitting back in the corner the night we went there after my arrival."

"Exactly. Do you want to try to find him, or shall I?"

"I'll let Gerald do it," Leon said. "He'd recognize him at once and would like a chance to get even. The human hurt him pretty badly."

"Fine," Chang said. "I'll tell Timothy to put a couple of security guards at your disposal. When you find this man, send him down to Camp T-3 and we'll find out what he knows."

Durk finished the last of his homemade whiskey and still wasn't satisfied. He'd spent the day working around the barn and house instead of in his fields. His tractor was still inaccessible, as he'd discovered when, after waking up late, he'd gone up to see if he could recover it. Crivit burrows surrounded it, tearing up his bean rows. They did not extend too far from the abandoned machine, but he dared not go over that ground to get it, especially since it was now out of fuel and would be hard to start. Even if he brought in a can of kerosene, the crivits' tentacles were long enough to reach him on the tractor's seat. And without the tractor, there wasn't much he could do.

Anxiety over the presence of the aliens next door added to his frustration. The result was that, after supper, he'd abandoned caution and drunk up the last of his moonshine. There hadn't been that much and he wanted more.

He went out to his truck, thinking that he could use it to haul his tractor in if the crivits weren't so active. If it would only rain, the ground would become inhospitable to the creatures, and it might be safe enough for him to hitch it up. But now the ground was drier than ever, the soil ever more permeable. Thank God, he thought as he started down the drive to the road, the clay made most of his farm inaccessible to the monsters.

The nearest place to get something to drink was the Five Star Bar. They weren't supposed to sell bottles of whiskey, but Tom Rogers knew Durk and maybe would make an exception. He drove the long way round so he wouldn't have to pass in front of the Thurston house.

The sunset was at its most spectacular when he pulled up into the parking lot in front of the bar. He recognized most of the cars there. He went in and saw Tom standing at the end of the bar, talking with George Monty.

"How's it going, Durk?" Tom asked.

"You don't want to know," Durk answered. "Evenin', George."

"Things been that bad, huh?" George asked.

"Moles," Durk said cryptically. "I need a bottle, Tom. Can you fix me up?"

Tom looked around at his other customers. "I guess so, if you keep it under your coat."

"I'd appreciate it. I'd rather not go all the way to Chapel Hill tonight."

"Churchill'd be closer, wouldn't it?" George asked.

"Than Chapel Hill but not closer than here. You want to come on down and help me work on it?"

"Man, you must be really desperate," George said as Tom went off to put a bottle of bourbon into a bag. "Sure, I'll keep you company."

"I'd appreciate it," Durk said. He took out his wallet and put a ten-dollar bill on the counter.

"That'll be six-twenty," Tom said, handing Durk the bag. He took the bill while Durk stuck the bag into his belt under his jacket and George finished up his beer. "You take it easy," Tom added when he brought back the change.

"I'll take it easy tomorrow," Durk said. "Thanks, Tom." He turned to the door just as it opened to admit three red-uniformed Visitors. One of them was Gerald.

"Oh, shit," Durk said, his voice a barely audible whisper. Gerald was looking right at him, a small smile on his artificial face.

"It's my turn now," Gerald said, his voice more resonant than ever. He stepped up and quickly swung a blow at Durk's midsection. Instead of hitting Durk's solar plexus, however, the Visitor's fist struck the bottle of bourbon with a sound of breaking knuckles.

Durk staggered back but did not lose his sudden opportunity. While Gerald was yelling and holding his injured hand and the other two Visitors hesitated in confusion, Durk turned and ran through the bar to the door at the back. Fortunately, nobody got in his way.

He went through the door with a crash, through the tiny office beyond, and out into the service area behind the bar. His truck was probably out of reach. He sprinted toward the woods beyond the bar and nearly made it when a powerful spotlight shone down from overhead, directly upon him. A laser pulse incinerated a spot in the ground right in the direction he was going.

He skidded to a stop, turning at the same time, but before he could make any headway in a different direction, another laser pulse struck just a yard away. Then a third. The shock of the near shots made him sit down heavily.

The spotlight centered on him. "Just hold it right there," an amplified voice called from overhead. Durk did not need to look up to know that an alien skyfighter was hovering above him. He heard the back door of the bar slam open and feet running toward him.

All the fight went out of him at once. He sat until the two soldiers who'd been with Gerald reached down to grab him and drag him roughly to his feet. One of them reached into his jacket and pulled out the bottle.

"This bar doesn't have a license for package sales," the Visitor said wryly. He and the other soldier, holding on to Durk's shoulders, marched him around to the front of the bar where the skyfighter was settling down to the pavement, blocking traffic. Gerald came out from the front, holding his broken hand.

"You're going to regret this, Mr. Attweiler," Gerald said. George or Tom must have told the Visitor Durk's name. Durk didn't blame them; they didn't want to be arrested too.

"Let's get him on board," Gerald told the two soldiers. The hatch of the skyfighter opened, and the soldiers forced Durk up the ramp.

Chapter 9

Durk Attweiler was processed into Camp T-3 just like any other human, except for a bit of first aid for the beating Gerald had given him *en route*. But unlike other humans, when he was put out into the compound, he recognized where he was.

It was night and lights shone down, not on the compound itself but onto the sandy moat that surrounded it outside the chain-link fence. That was different, but the barracks buildings were the same as when Durk had been here before. Back then, this had been a part of the Fort Bragg military base.

There were few other prisoners up and about at this time of night. Durk had no instructions from his captors as to where to go or what to do with himself, so he went to where a small group of people was standing at a darkened corner of one of the barracks.

"Excuse me," he said, "but where can I find a place to sleep?"

"They got you too," an older man said, turning to face him. It was Professor Morton Barnes.

"Welcome to Camp T-3," a young man with wildly disheveled hair said sardonically. "You too can become some lizard's lunch."

"Be quiet, Peter," a black man said. "Our new friend might prove himself useful to our hosts in other ways."

"It is to be hoped," Professor Barnes said. "Durk Attweiler, meet Peter Frye and Cliff Upton."

"Are you badly hurt?" Upton asked, noticing Durk's bandages.

"Not as badly as the guy who beat me is," Durk said. "He was angry, but he wasn't tough enough to do me any real damage."

"They don't want to spoil their livestock," Peter said, pursuing a dark thought.

"Enough, Peter," Upton said again. "We don't know that that's what's in store for us."

"Like hell we don't," Peter said. "You know what this place is, Attweiler? It's a stockyard. If we can't be made into slaves, or if we don't throw ourselves to the crivits outside the fence, we're all going to be eaten. How do you like that?"

Upton slapped him across the face. Peter didn't strike back but just turned away, his hands clenched into fists.

"Don't pay any attention to him," Barnes said. "He's just overwrought."

"No, he isn't," Durk said. "He's probably got the situation pretty well figured out. But do you? Have the lizards questioned you much?"

"No, not much. What do you mean?"

"Have they asked you about certain people you know? About Dr. Van Oort, for example?"

"Uh, no, not that I know of. Why?"

"Because," Durk said, "if they do, they'll find out all about what those people are doing. I don't want to die, Professor Barnes, and maybe they just think I'm a trespasser. But if they start to get too close to what I know about crivits and what other people are learning about them, I may have to decide to go take a walk across that sand over there, just so they won't pick my brains. Have you thought about that?"

"Jesus," Barnes said.

* * *

It was nearly midnight in the secret lab below Data Tronix. Bill Gray punched a global-search command into the console. The screen overhead showed the word, "SEARCHING."

Next to him, Paul Freedman was running another program to compile a series of reports based on internal communications intercepted at Visitor headquarters. These communications all had to do with the Visitors' attempts at monitoring human activities in the Research Triangle Park. From these reports, extrapolations could be made to indicate which of the various research facilities were currently under the most intense surveillance and which, as a consequence, should be most careful about their own activities and communications. Those who for the moment were being ignored could afford to take chances. Since the development of this system, the two dozen companies in the Park had been able to operate more freely than they had in the past, whether their activities were directly opposed to Visitor regulations or of just marginal interest to the aliens.

Bill's screen scrolled and now read:

SEARCH STRING "CAMP T-3" FOUND. FOUR ENTRIES.

TYPE "R" TO READ, "P" TO PRINT, "S" TO STORE TO DISK.

Bill typed "R". The entries were all very brief. The third one, however, made him pause.

SPEAKER A: We have the human Durk Attweiler in custody and are now on our way to Camp T-3.

SPEAKER B: Very good, Gerald. I hope you didn't hurt him too badly.

SPEAKER A: Just a little bit. Any special instructions?

SPEAKER B: Just make sure he'll be able to talk when we want him to.

SPEAKER A: Don't worry about that.

"Look at this," Bill said to Paul. "Wasn't it Durk Attweiler who took Mark and Anne and those down to bug the crivit ranch?"

"That's right," Paul said. "We'd better let them know about this."

"Won't do them any good if we can't find out where Camp T-3 is."

"That message sounds like it was being transmitted from a skyfighter. Run a triangulation on it."

"Right," Bill said. He canceled the rest of the report and called up another program. Feeding it the ID code of the message in question, he got the data on signal strength and direction from the time it was intercepted.

"Looks like somewhere near Fayetteville," he said.

"Fort Bragg," Paul said. "I'll bet you anything that's where Camp T-3 is, somewhere out on their artillery range."

"Goddamn it, I bet you're right." He reached for the dedicated phone whose only other connection was to Anne Marino's office. She answered it immediately.

"Durk Attweiler has been taken to Camp T-3," Bill said without preamble, "and we think that's somewhere in Fort Bragg."

"Who's with you?" Anne asked.

"Paul."

"Okay, put everything on auto and come on up."

"Right." He hung up and turned to Paul. "I think we're going to see some action," he said. "Let's go."

They went up the elevator to the second floor, and from there to Anne's office. They met Lester Ortega on the way. Mark Casey was already there when they arrived.

"Are you sure it's Fort Bragg?" was the first thing Mark asked them as they came in.

"No," Bill said, "but it fits the other data very well. We had the range, but not the direction, and that call from the skyfighter gave us that. Fort Bragg, about the middle of the artillery range should be about right."

"What kind of facilities did the Army have down there?" Anne asked.

"A special set of barracks for exercises," Paul said. "There's a lot of sand too."

"Perfect for crivits," Mark said. "Except you'd think they'd take over the whole base."

"Probably have some kind of undersand fencing," Lester said. "But so what? Are we going to rescue this Attweiler?"

"We'll have to, and Professor Barnes as well," Anne said. "As to so what, if the crivits are confined to a sand moat, that's one thing. If they've been allowed the run of the base, we couldn't come within a mile of the place."

"Everything we've heard so far," Paul said, "indicates that the Visitors don't like to let the crivits have too much freedom. Seems to me that was one of the complaints Diana made about Leon's project—lack of crivit security."

"Okay," Mark said, "so we'll just have to assume the crivits are kept under control. But we're still going to have to locate Camp T-3 more precisely and figure out some way not only of getting to it but of getting people out."

"As to the first," Anne said, turning to Paul, "how well do you know Fort Bragg?"

"I worked there for two years," Paul answered. "If Camp T-3 is where I think it is, I can lead you right to it."

"Good. And as to the second—" Her phone rang. She answered it, and when the person on the other end spoke, she smiled. "Couldn't be better timing," she said. "As to the second," she repeated as she hung up, "that was word that professional help is on the way. Bill, go over to the airport right now. We've got some friends coming in from Los Angeles."

The wait for Bill Gray to return seemed interminable. In the meantime Anne got hold of Jack Corey and asked him and Wendel Fenister to meet them at the courthouse in Pittsboro, which was on the way to Fayetteville. Mark went off to scare up whatever equipment might prove useful. Paul Freedman went home to get maps of Fort Bragg which he'd saved from when he'd worked at their computer facility there some years ago. And Lester Ortega went over to Diger-Fairwell to let Dr. Lucia Van Oort know what was happening. Everybody had come back to Anne's offices before Bill returned from the airport.

When he finally arrived, he had three people with him. Everybody recognized the large but graceful figure of Chris Faber, though it had been nearly two years since Ham Tyler's henchman had been seen on TV in his role as a freedom fighter in Los Angeles. The other two were completely unknown.

"This is Grace Delaney," Chris said, introducing a strong, hard woman, "and Fred Linker," a slender man who looked too soft to be of much help. "Two of the toughest people you're ever likely to meet, short of The Fixer himself. We don't have much of the picture, other than that your espionage efforts here are in danger if this guy Barnes is made to talk. Can you fill us in?"

"Let's do that on the way down," Anne said. "The sooner we get on the road, the better chance of success we'll have."

"That's right," Grace said. "Chris's movements are pretty hard to conceal, and the lizards will know he's somewhere in the area before the day is out."

"All right then," Chris said, "let's move."

They took three cars for the eight people, and thirty minutes later met Jack Corey and a rapidly recovering Wendel Fenister, who were in a car of their own, in the small town of Pittsboro, sixteen miles south of Chapel Hill. From there it was another hour to Fayetteville.

Paul, in the lead car, led them south around the city and along a state highway that ran east and west on the south edge of the military base. They took a side road north onto the base until the pavement ended at an abandoned barrier. Chris got out to make sure that the drop bar was not connected to any signaling device and then raised it by hand. They drove through onto a dirt road leading into the heart of the base.

By the time Paul got them to where they could see the lights of the camp, it was just an hour before dawn. Chris, Grace, and Fred opened the luggage they'd brought down with them and distributed small but powerful machine pistols and ammunition. Then they moved through the scraggly pines toward the camp.

"Be careful," Mark said as they neared the edge of the trees, beyond which was the sand moat. "There are crivits in there. They—"

"I know all about them," Chris said. "This isn't the first prison camp I've had experience with." He looked out at the barracks buildings just beyond the fence. "We can't go in here," he said. "But the lizards have to have some means of access."

"How about over there?" Lester suggested, pointing to the left where a second, smaller compound adjoined the larger one.

"Good for you," Chris said. "Most of their prisoners would come in by flyer, landing on that roof there, but the lizard staff themselves will have some kind of walkway, and that's where it's likely to be."

They worked their way around through the trees until they could see the front of the building at the side of the secondary compound. Sure enough, a broad paved road led right up to the front door.

"But won't they have guards in there?" Mark asked.

"Of course they will," Grace said. "But it's like any castle. It's impenetrable on all sides except where the door is, and that's where the guardhouse is, because it's not impenetrable."

"Makes sense," Bill muttered, though it didn't to him. "So what do we do, shoot our way in?"

"Unless you can rig a bridge across that moat," Chris said, "that's exactly what we do."

Everybody except Grace and Fred were appalled by the idea. Even Jack Corey, who'd seen combat in Vietnam, wasn't thrilled at the prospect. "We could get killed in there," he said simply, not protesting but just stating a fact.

"We could," Fred Linker said. "And nobody has to go in who doesn't want to. But the information you people have gotten out of the Visitor headquarters up at the Park has

been very useful. More lives than our own might be at
stake, at least those who Barnes and Attweiler could name
as being involved in the espionage."

"So how do we do it?" Lester Ortega asked.

"First we blow the door," Grace said.

"No," Anne interrupted. "First I pick the lock."

"That's better," Chris said. "Then Paul, you know the
building, you and I lead the way through to the main
compound."

"And then?" Mark asked.

"Then either we break them out or we die trying."

Without any more conversation, Anne went up to the
door and knelt down to examine the lock. She reached into
an inside jacket pocket and took out what looked like a fat
wallet. Inside were her collection of lockpicks. The others
couldn't see what she was doing, other than that she
selected something, fiddled with the lock a moment, put it
back, and got out another tool and tried again. She put that
one away and stood up from her crouch.

"Didn't it work?" Chris asked.

"Of course it worked," Anne said. "I didn't spend four
years at Caltech for nothing." She put her hand on the knob
and the door swung open.

Now it was Paul's turn to take charge. With the others
following, Paul led them through a more than typical foyer,
down a hall past several closed doors, and into a room
where large doors opened on either side.

"This is where the prisoners would be brought in," Paul
said. "That door there, the one on the left, leads up to the
copter pad on the roof, which is where the skyfighters
would land. The door on the right goes to other parts of the
building, but this one," he pointed to the one opposite the
door by which they had entered, "should go straight back
through to the compound, if they haven't changed things
around any."

"Where are the guards?" Grace Delaney asked. She and
Fred Linker were sharply alert, but not nervous, as Bill,
Mark, and Anne were. Jack and Wendel seemed calm.

"I don't know," Paul said, "but they could be anywhere. This used to be a ready room."

"The only thing we can do," Chris said, "is to go through and be prepared to fight. Will you know this guy Barnes when you see him?"

"Yes," Anne said, "and Attweiler too." She checked to make sure that her machine pistol was off safety, as did the others. "Let's do it," she said.

Paul opened the door. Beyond was another corridor with no other doors except the one at the far end. Tense with apprehension, they went down it and found the far door locked. Once again Anne got out her lockpicks while the others kept alert for any signs of discovery. This lock proved as easy to open as the other had been.

Beyond this door was another room where there were three guards. Their expressions of surprise indicated they had expected only friends instead of the ten grim humans with drawn guns.

"Don't even squeak," Chris warned the three Visitors, who raised their hands in surrender. Grace and Fred quickly went to work tying them to their chairs.

"We thought you were our relief," one of the guards said. "They're due right about now."

"We'll deal with them when they come," Chris told him.

When the guards were secured, Fred and Grace stood on either side of the door to the compound, facing into the room to meet the relief when they came. Jack and Wendel took positions by the inner doors to listen for the sounds of approach. Under Anne and Chris's direction, Paul, Lester, and Bill went through into the compound itself to stand watch outside the door while Chris stood in the now open doorway to lend aid wherever it would be needed.

There were no guards in the compound, but there were a few prisoners walking around in the gray of early morning. They did not notice Mark and Anne at first as they crossed the barren ground to the nearest of the barracks buildings. Then one of them, a tall black man, turned to stare and said softly, "It's a breakout."

"Where is Morton Barnes?" Anne asked him urgently. "And Durk Attweiler?"

"They're both over in building C," the man said. "You got time for the rest of us?"

"We'll free as many as we can," Mark said as he and Anne hurried toward the indicated barracks, with the black man beside them, "but those two know things that can endanger hundreds, maybe thousands of people if the lizards get them to talk."

"I understand," the man said. He looked back over his shoulder where he could see Paul, Bill, and Chris still at the door of the compound entrance. "We'd better move. They change guards about now."

"So the lizards inside told us," Anne said. They came to the door of building C and went inside. The black man pushed past them and went to a bunk halfway down the long room.

"Professor Barnes," he said softly, shaking the sleeping man's shoulder. "Get up and be quiet. We're going to break out."

Barnes roused quickly, looked around the room until he saw Mark and Anne, and then got out of bed.

"You too, Cliff?" he asked as he pulled on his pants and shoes.

"Everybody who can make it," Mark said. Cliff Upton went on to the far end of the room where Durk Attweiler was already getting up. Several other people had awakened as well.

"Get everybody up and moving," Anne told those who were awake. "Get the other barracks alerted and head toward the main entrance."

Barnes went across the center aisle and aroused a short, muscular young man. "Peter, get up, we're breaking out," he said. Peter Frye just snarled.

"Sure," he said, his voice thick with sleep. "Tell me how." He rolled over as if he didn't want to hear the answer.

Barnes started to go to other bunks, but Mark took his shoulder. "They'll have to come on their own," he told the professor. "You and Durk Attweiler here," he nodded at the farmer, who was coming up to join them, "are the ones we really want."

"We know too much," Durk said in answer to Barnes's questioning look.

Cliff Upton had sent others off to notify the other barracks, and now he came back to join Mark and Anne and the others. "Let's make tracks," he said. "The relief guards are overdue—"

And that's when the shooting started.

Mark and Anne grabbed Barnes and Attweiler and hurried toward the door, with Cliff Upton close behind them. The others were now frantically getting out of bed and dressed. Peter Frye rolled over, stared at the ceiling, then rolled back facedown on his bed.

From the door of the barracks, with people pressing behind them, they could see Paul and Bill crouched in the doorway of the compound entrance, firing into the room beyond. There was no sign of Chris Faber. Mark and Anne hurried their charges across the barren ground, which was rapidly filling with other prisoners, mostly confused, but some also running toward the exit. Paul saw them coming, spoke to Bill, and the two stood to enter the guard room ahead of the others. When Mark and Anne got there, the battle had moved inward.

The three guards were dead in their chairs, caught in the crossfire. The sounds of shots came from several directions inside the building, but Anne didn't pay any heed. Those who were fighting had their jobs to do. It was Anne's responsibility to get Barnes and Attweiler out of the prison camp.

They went up the hall to the ready room where they found Grace Delaney wounded and Jack Corey keeping other Visitors from entering. They fired rapid single shots until the escapees entered. Then Grace put her pistol on full automatic. Mark and Anne also fired, blindly, through doorways on either side as they crossed the room. More shots came from ahead of them.

Paul came up beside them while Bill helped Grace to her feet. Cliff Upton had picked up a Visitor weapon and was taking shots at whatever moved. Other prisoners, some now also armed, poured into the ready room behind them.

To Anne and Mark, the details of the next few minutes were never clear. They remembered shooting and ducking, and unarmed prisoners throwing themselves through doorways and dragging out screaming red-uniformed guards. They remembered movement, shouts, a turmoil of humans overwhelming the Visitors by sheer force of numbers. They remembered Paul going down with a hole in his forehead, Jack and Wendel moving as if stalking deer, and the bulk of Chris Faber, who now seemed to be everywhere, moving gracefully and steadily, directing the breakout as if he knew what he was doing.

And then suddenly they were outside the building and running for the trees. Other Visitors from other buildings were running, shooting, shouting, but the stream of prisoners from the compound would not be stopped. Many humans went down. But many Visitors fell as well.

Then for a while it was a long run through the trees, toward the parked cars. Behind them were the sounds of the escape growing more distant. Bill and Grace were the last to arrive, with Cliff Upton covering their rear.

"Everybody in and let's move," Chris said, sorting people into cars. The engines revved and they were away.

Chapter 10

Dr. Lucia Van Oort was just about to go up to the cafeteria for lunch when Penny Carmichal came into her office.

"We've misinterpreted this whole crivit business," Penny said. "As much of a problem they would be if they were released into the contryside, they're nothing compared to what would happen if these other animals were set loose."

"The verlogs?" Lucia asked. "But they're just vegetarians."

"So were the rabbits in Australia," Penny said. "And think about plagues of locusts that can strip square miles of vegetation right down to the ground. These verlogs breed quickly, with large litters, eat almost any plant life that exists in massive quantities, and get this—they have no known predators—except crivits."

"Good God! You mean Leon has been breeding crivits just to keep the verlogs under control?"

"That's what it looks like. The verlogs are the Visitors' main source of protein. Our animals, and humans, are just extra. Verlogs are to Visitors what beef and pork are to us. As near as I can figure, Leon plans to let the verlogs loose with the crivits to keep their population under control. But it won't work. The crivits can't climb trees. They can't cross ground that is too hard. The verlogs would eventually overwhelm the whole East Coast, and then the rest of the country. By the time they'd overbred and started dying of starvation, so would everybody and everything else."

"That means that Mark is after the wrong target," Lucia said.

"Have they already started?" Penny asked.

"About an hour ago. Durk Attweiler volunteered to go down with them, even though they'd been back from Fort Bragg only two hours."

"You don't suppose they'd let the verlogs loose by accident," Penny said, knowing full well that that was almost certain to happen.

"We've got to warn them," Lucia said. "Killing crivits is all right, but, damn, the verlogs *must* be destroyed." She got on the phone and called over to Anne Marino's office at Data Tronix. Anne was not in, but Steve Wong took her call.

"We've got to abort Project Silicon," Lucia said urgently, heedless of being overheard.

"But they've already set off," Steve said.

"I know, but you've got to stop them. I can't explain— uh, it's not the wolves, it's the rabbits, do you understand?"

"Wait a minute. Okay, right, not the target but the other thing."

"Exactly," Lucia said, hoping he really did understand it was verlogs and not crivits that she was referring to. "Think of a plague of locusts," she said, taking Penny's analogy. "With no predators."

"Holy shit," Steve said, and now Lucia knew that he did in fact understand. "It was staring us in the face all the time, and we never saw it. And we've gotten further information that— Oh, my God, if those figures mean what I think they mean, the rabbits could eat the country to the ground within ten years."

"No good for anybody if that happens," Lucia said in complete understatement. "Do something, Steve, before it's too late."

* * *

Steve hung up, numb with the realization of what the verlogs could do if they escaped from the crivit ranch. Japanese beetles could destroy a rose bush in a week. Gypsy moths could strip trees in a month. Rabbits in Australia almost caused the collapse of their economy, and did severe damage to their ecology for years. And verlogs—he shook himself out of his nightmarish reverie and went looking for Anne Marino.

He found her in a meeting of division supervisors—after all, Data Tronix had its regular work to attend to—and barged in without apology.

"Anne," he said, ignoring the others present, "we've got big trouble, and I've got to talk to you *right now*!"

They left without any explanation; that would have to come later. Out in the hall, Steve told her about Dr. Van Oort's phone call and what it implied. Anne understood immediately.

"All right," she said, "if we hurry, we may be able to catch them before they attack the crivit ranch."

They went down to her car, and Anne broke as many traffic laws as she dared on her way south to Durk Attweiler's farm. Other cars were in the barn, but there was no sign of the attackers.

"You stay here," she told Steve, "just in case they haven't started yet and come back. But if you hear shooting—"

"I know, then I'll take word to them the best way I can."

"Right. I'm going to try to head them off."

She got back in her car and drove around to the road on the far side of the crivit ranch. She pulled off onto the shoulder and started cross-country toward the old mine head. She was sure she could find it, even in the woods, since it was on the hill that lay between her and the Thurston place. It was only a mile away, but though she ran, it seemed to take forever.

She topped the ridge at last and saw that she was a bit too far to the north. From here, she could see the Thurston buildings, the barns, and the enclosure around the crivit feeding area. The mine head was to her left.

She ran toward it, heedless of the fact that she was plainly visible to Visitors in red down at the farm. She ignored their shouts but fell to her knees at the entrance to the mine and peered down into the darkness. Mark and Chris, at the foot of the ladder below, looked up at her, surprised.

"Thank God," Anne said, calling down to them even as they started up the ladder, with Grace, Fred, Durk, Jack, and Wendel close behind. "Forget the crivits," she said, "it's the verlogs we've got to destroy."

"You've blown our cover," Chris said as he poked his head up out of the ground. Several Visitors were now coming up the slope through the woods toward them.

"If those verlogs escape," Anne said, "they'll eat this country right down to the ground." She pointed to the trees within the not so distant feeding enclosure. All were bare, and even the twigs were gone.

"Damn," Chris said, getting out of the way so Mark could come up. Then the Visitors started firing.

Chris and Mark returned the fire, allowing the rest of the invasion party to come up out of the mine while Anne tried to explain the significance of the verlogs and the need for her to have spoiled the attack and put them all in danger.

"It makes sense in a funny kind of way," Grace Delaney said between shots. "The lizards know even less about protecting their environment than we do, and a stunt like that is just the kind of thing they might pull."

Jack and Wendel had both worked farms, and both understood what an unhindered pest invasion could do to crops. They did not need much imagination, after seeing the destroyed trees in the crivit feeding area, to picture what the whole countryside would look like if the verlogs were set loose. Even Mark and Chris could get the picture, though they were busy along with the others in keeping the Visitors down the hill at bay.

"They're going to have reinforcements pretty soon,"

Fred Linker said, dodging laser shots. "Maybe we should just run for it."

"My farm would be the first place those verlogs would eat," Durk Attweiler protested. "Running away won't do me any good at all."

"So what are you going to do?" Fred asked. "Walk down there and kill them all?"

"Something like that," Durk said. But his words seemed foolish, because the Visitors were working ever closer. Leon was not among them, but there were more than the regular staff. And all, in spite of their ostensible occupations, were experienced soldiers. Slowly, the invaders had to give way.

"What you need is a good fire," Chris said to Durk. "A bomb would blow the verlog barn apart, but some of them might escape."

"What are you talking about?" Fred said. "We can come back and clean them up another time."

"You think Leon's going to wait for us?" Mark snapped, then had to duck as a Visitor energy bolt struck the tree near his head, sending fragments of bark and wood flying. "Diana's never approved of his experiment, and once she gets word of this attack, she'll close him down. The only way he can finish his experiment is to release the verlogs right now."

And then there was no time for further argument, because the reinforcements Fred had predicted arrived. The sky-fighters settled down in the clear space next to the house, and ten heavily armed Visitor soldiers emerged.

"Looks like we don't have any choice," Anne said. "Durk, we'll have to come back—" But Durk was gone.

"Spread out through the trees," Chris said. "We can't get back to Attweiler's; we'll have to hitch rides on the highway."

"Those of us who make it alive," Fred said.

The group split and retreated through the trees toward the east.

* * *

Durk crawled on his belly through a briar patch, ignoring the thorns that tore at his arms and back. The Visitors passed within yards of his position, but the dense foliage of the blackberry canes concealed him from their distracted view. When he could move again, he continued crawling, still clutching the machine pistol Chris had given him before going down into the mine entrance at the riverbank.

Fire was what was needed, and he thought he knew where he could get it—the kerosene tank against the north end of the verlog barn. If there was any kerosene left in it. Still, it was worth a try. He moved along the crest of the ridge, away from the now retreating battle, until he could see the tank through the trees on the slope. It was two hundred yards away.

And then his eyes caught a movement beyond the house. Someone, a man, a human, was coming from the direction of his place. It was Steve Wong.

Durk got to his feet and half ran down the slope, making only a token effort at concealment. Steve saw him, glanced at the house, and ran to meet him by the kerosene tank.

"Anne got to you then," Steve said.

"She did," Durk answered. "They're fighting a retreat toward the highway. But we've got to do something about these verlogs."

"You're telling me." He grabbed a stanchion supporting the tank and shook it. There was a barely audible sloshing sound from inside.

"Let's hope it's enough," Durk said.

"How do we get it into the barn?" Steve asked. The only windows were at the back of the barn, beyond reach of the short filler hose. Durk took his pistol and, aiming low, shot off the clip, ripping a hole in the wall. Then he took the filler hose and stuck it into the hole. He squeezed the release valve, and wedged a splinter of wood into the trigger to hold it open. Kerosene gurgled out of the tank into the barn.

And a door slammed at the house just out of sight.

"Leon," Durk said. He stuffed a new clip into the gun

while Steve, unarmed, dropped to his knees to peer around the corner of the barn.

"It is indeed," Steve said, quickly getting to his feet and pressing close to the barn wall. "And he's armed and coming this way."

"Get ready to light the kerosene," Durk said. "I'll hold him off." He took Steve's place at the corner of the barn, peered around, and ducked back as Leon fired. The shot splintered the corner of the barn just inches from his face. He stuck his pistol around the corner and aiming by guess let off a short burst. His only satisfaction was hearing Leon scramble.

"I can't get it lit," Steve cried, half panicked. Up on the ridge above the barn, three or four Visitors were coming back, having heard Durk's fusillade.

"You can't light it like that," Durk said, turning to see Steve touch a lit match to a rivulet of kerosene. The fluid just put the match out. He strode past to the far side, ripped off a few shots at the approaching soldiers, then came back to Steve and handed him the pistol and two extra clips.

"You keep them busy," he said. Then, while Steve moved from one corner to the other, firing alternately from each position, Durk took out his wallet. Inside were five singles, a ten, and a twenty. He crumpled them up into a big wad and put it into the kerosene. Slowly, the fuel soaked into the money. Only then did he light a match and touch it to the wad of currency which now acted like a wick. He pushed this now burning mass into the hole in the side of the barn.

"It will take a few minutes to get going," he said, "but the whole floor is covered with kerosene, and when it goes nothing inside will survive."

"Then let's get out of here," Steve started to say when a laser bolt took him high in the chest and he went down.

Durk threw himself on the ground and crawled to Steve, but the man was dead. Coldly, Durk retrieved the pistol from Steve's clenched fist, plugged in the last of the ammunition clips, and prepared himself to take out as many of his attackers as he could before he himself was gunned down.

The soldiers coming down the slope were overly confident. Durk, with years of experience in picking off squirrels and rabbits as they ran, dropped all three with three short bursts. But there was still Leon to deal with, and other soldiers were coming back now, having given up on the fleeing humans.

Thick, black, oily smoke began to leak out of the hole in the barn wall and from other places around the other sides of the building. The kerosene, burning poorly from lack of adequate air, was producing huge quantities of noxious smoke and gas which, alone, would kill all the verlogs inside.

Durk went toward the front of the barn and cautiously looked around the corner to see Leon who, concerned more for his animals than for Durk, was frantically trying to open the newly locked front doors. Durk just smiled and backed away. When Leon at last succeeded and threw the doors open, smoke in a dense, black cloud billowed from the entrance, and the sudden influx of air caused the kerosene to ignite completely. The effect was like a soft explosion, with gouts of red flame bursting from the double door and from the eaves of the roof and blowing out the windows at the back of the barn. Leon was knocked over backward, and the soldiers in the woods all started shouting.

A moment's confusion was all Durk needed. He ran from the barn toward the back of the Thurston house and his own property beyond. He heard Leon yelling just as he rounded the corner of the house, and Visitor weapons fired at him uselessly.

But he didn't go straight toward his house. He'd run from revenuers before, and his instincts took charge now. Instead, he went north around the feeding enclosure and up the side of the fence that kept the crivits confined to the channel to their sand pits. Behind him he could hear the sounds of running feet and more shots.

He ran through the trees now, diagonally across the side

of Thurston's farm, until he burst from the woods at the fence opposite where his tractor still stood in his bean field. The ground was all furrowed with crivit burrows, and even as he climbed the fence, Durk could see other burrows being freshly made. He ran across his own field toward the tractor, leaping the burrows, dodging the Visitors' fire. He could hear Leon behind him, shouting. That was just fine.

Two crivits, plowing through the soil their previous burrows had made loose, tunneled after him just below the surface. Durk made it to his tractor, climbed on and over, and crouched behind the engine, just above the ground. The crivits, confused when he left the ground, circled around, and one raised a tentacle tentatively into the air, just a few yards from him.

The body of the tractor protected him from the Visitors' shots. With one leg hooked over his gearshift and his head up against the front of the tractor, Durk looked back the way he had come and watched as Leon and three other soldiers came out of the woods and across his field toward him. They knew where he was all right, and there was nowhere Durk could run.

But the crivits, frustrated at missing him, felt the vibrations in the soil made by the running Visitors. Before Leon and his soldiers had crossed half the distance to the tractor, four moving mounds of broken earth converged on them. Durk laughed as eight tentacles reached up into the air to grab the red-uniformed Visitors and dragged them down, screaming, into the loose soil. The ground roiled for a moment, and then was still.

And Durk, with the crivits now satisfied, stepped down to the ground and walked away.

Watch for

THE NEW ENGLAND RESISTANCE

next in the V series
from Pinnacle Books

coming in June!

YOU WATCHED IT ON TV...

NOW
DISCOVER
THE STARTLING
TRUTH
BEHIND
THE
INVASION...

...as the ultimate battle
for survival continues...

DOCTOR WHO

More bestselling science fiction from Pinnacle, America's #1 series publisher!